MARCIE and the SHRIMP BOAT ADVENTURE

BETTY HAGER

ZondervanPublishingHouse
Grand Rapids, Michigan

A Division of HarperCollinsPublishers

Marcie and the Shrimp Boat Adventure
Copyright © 1994 by Betty Hager

Requests for information should be addressed to:
Zondervan Publishing House
Grand Rapids, Michigan 49530

Library of Congress Cataloging-in-Publication Data

Hager, Betty.
      Marcie and the shrimp boat adventure / Betty Hager.
         p.   cm. — (Tales from the bayou)
      Summary: Eleven-year-old Marcie accompanies her brother
and their Cajun friend Jake on a shrimping expedition whose
near-tragic end teaches Marcie about more important things than
shrimping.
      ISBN 0-310-38421-4 (paper)
      [1. Fishing — Fiction. 2. Boats and boating — Fiction.
3. Cajuns — Fiction. 4. Conduct of life — Fiction. 5. Brothers
and sisters — Fiction. 6. Race relations — Fiction.] I. Title.
II. Series: Hager, Betty. Tales from the bayou.
      PZ7.H12416Mat   1994   93–44488
      [Fic] — dc20   CIP
                                                          AC

Edited by Lori J. Walburg
Cover designed by Cindy Davis
Cover illustration by Doug Knutson
Interior illustrations by Craig Wilson, the Comark Group

Printed in the United States of America

94 95 96 97 98 99 / ❖DH/ 10 9 8 7 6 5 4 3 2 1

For Chris,
Chris, and Molly,
because I love them

Contents

A One-Track Mind

More than anything else, I wanted to go shrimping.

Shrimpers made good money, for one thing. Once, when my big brother Raymie was fourteen, he went shrimping for the whole month of August and made ninety-five dollars. For a while he thought he was rich, and so did I. With that much money, I could have a chocolate soda every day for at least a month.

Besides, nothing seemed more glamorous to me than shrimping. Many a morning I'd sit on the great, gnarled roots of the big oak across the road from our house. There I'd watch the shrimp boats go by, on their way out to the Gulf of Mexico. Against a startling blue sky, the white boats were beautiful. The graceful curve of them, their tar-blackened masts, the sun-browned, muscular shoulders of the working men—all these sights thrilled me.

Sometimes boys went out shrimping with their daddies. But in the mid 1930s in Bayou La Batre, Alabama, not many people had heard of a *girl* going out on a shrimp boat—especially not an eleven-year-old girl like me.

But I was determined to go.

One January afternoon I took my latest library book down to the bayou to read on the wharf. Papa was outside his hardware store working on the gas pumps, and I spread out my throw rug not far away. I had just settled in to read when Mr. Tolly Breame came up.

"Hey, Isaac, how are you?" he greeted Papa.

"Afternoon, Tolly," Papa said.

Mr. Tolly ran the ice plant in town. That's where we got the ice blocks to put in our iceboxes to keep our meat and vegetables cold. The fishermen bought tons of it to keep their seafood fresh.

"You know, Isaac," Mr. Tolly said, "I've got this friend, Billy Jim Boisonot, who's moving to Bayou La Batre from Mississippi."

Mr. Tolly leaned on the gas pump and watched as Papa worked. "Billy Jim says he's gonna be so busy moving, he's not gonna have much time to shrimp when the season starts. So he's looking for someone who might like to use his boat. And I thought of that fella, Jake, who lives out back of your house. He could earn some good money for a while taking Billy Jim's boat out for him."

I put my book down and sat up.

Papa said, "Why, that's mighty nice of you to be thinking of him, Tolly, but Jake has a bad back."

Mr. Tolly clucked his tongue sympathetically and said, "My gracious, I didn't know that."

"Yeah," Papa said, shaking his head. "He hurt it when he was shrimping over in Louisiana. As much as he'd appreciate the money, frankly, Tolly, I'm not sure he's up to doing the job."

I couldn't help it. I just had to put my two cents in. I jumped up and tugged at Papa's sleeve.

"Well, it couldn't hurt him to ask, Papa," I squeaked. My voice did that when I was excited.

Papa seemed a bit irritated with me, but Mr. Tolly grinned and said, "She's right, Isaac. We oughta give the man a chance to speak for himself."

Now that I had someone on my side I had more wisdom to add. "If Mr. Jake had a strong crew to help him, he could just be the boss," I suggested. "He wouldn't have to do the heavy work. The crew could do that."

I had at least one person in mind for the job. Me.

Papa lifted an eyebrow at me and smiled that "knowing" smile of his. He knew I had set my heart on going shrimping. I'd been bugging Mama and him about it for months. But all they did about it was shake their heads and say, "My, Marcie, but you do have a one-track mind."

"Marcie, sweetheart, you have the right idea, but a crew would take real strong *men*, you know," Papa said, grinning at me.

11

I scowled at him. *Honestly,* I thought, *Papa doesn't realize how strong I am. He thinks just 'cause I'm a girl I couldn't be a part of a shrimp boat crew. If he'd give me the chance, I'd show him.*

But I didn't say anything out loud. I knew better than to say anything. Mr. Tolly might laugh if I said just who I had in mind.

Papa looked at my face. His eyes twinkled. "All right, Marcie," he said. "Why don't you run and ask Mr. Jake what he thinks?"

My face lit up. "Yes, sir!" I said.

I raced across the white shell road to our house. I could see Mr. Jake hoeing in his little garden behind our house. I was so anxious to get to him I stumbled over the strings he was tying on the tomatoes.

He looked up and smiled. *"Comment ca va, Mam'selle?"* he said.

I got up, brushed the dirt from my knees, and tried to undo the damage I had done to the tomato string.

"De young lady in big, big hurry, *n'est ce pas*?" Mr. Jake said in his quaint Cajun accent, sprinkled with French. He smiled at me. I never saw Mr. Jake's eyes crinkled up in a smile that I didn't think of how Raymie and I had once thought he was some sort of evil ghost. We sure had been wrong about him.

I gave him a weak grin, looking at the tangled string in despair.

"Iss all right, little wan," he said. He took the string from me and quietly tied it back in place.

I started telling Mr. Jake about Mr. Tolly, and somebody named Billy Jim from Mississippi, and his shrimp boat, and, well, just about anything else I could remember.

Mr. Jake looked at me, puzzled. It was obvious I hadn't made sense. Then I realized. I never did make sense when I was excited. I started over and repeated Mr. Tolly's and Papa's conversation as clearly as I could.

At first, Mr. Jake's eyes were dark and sad.

"Ah, Missy Marcie, Mr. Isaac, he right, you know. De back no good. Bad, bad. I can hoe de garden, yes. But fishing . . . throwing de net, hauling it up when it fill with de shrimp, dat take much, much strength."

I caught his arm and turned so I could look into his eyes. "Yeah, but listen," I said, "I have a terrific idea. Raymie and I could be your crew."

I didn't like the way he grinned, the same grin Papa had when he thought I was being a "cute little girl." I tried to keep my irritation from showing.

"Really, Mr. Jake," I said, my voice shrill with excitement, "I know Papa would let Raymie go for a while, 'cause we'll be off for Easter vacation. And we . . . we're *strong*. Honest. Just look at my muscles."

I held up my forearm and clenched my fist to show the bulge. I was proud of the muscles I'd built up rowing on the bayou. As skinny as I was, I had muscles.

"Yeah," Mr. Jake breathed a sigh of what I believed to be genuine admiration, "but even if de muscle, dey be big, big, your mama never let her little girl go on de shrimp boat, *ma petite mam'selle*."

I ignored what he said, because just then another brilliant idea came to me, ripe and ready for the picking. "Raymie's friend Hank could go, too," I said. "He's *really* strong."

I knew I hadn't convinced him about me, but I could see his eyes light up like two flashlights. He was interested, all right.

Before he could say anything, I was off running. "I'll tell Papa you'll think about it!" I called over my shoulder.

Back at the hardware store, I waited impatiently while Papa talked with a customer. As soon as we had the shop to ourselves, I told him what Mistuh Jake had said, and my idea about Raymie, Hank, and me being the crew.

Papa opened up a box and started shelving cans of oil. "Honey," he said as he worked, "you know how terrible a load of shrimp smells? Besides, you always seem to disappear when Mama wants you to help pick them for cooking."

Defensively, I said, "Well, those sharp little edges cut my fingers."

Papa gave me one of those Papa-knows-the-truth looks.

"How'd you like to handle a few hundred pounds of those little creatures? Remember how you scream when Raymie threatens to put one down your back, or just make you hold one?"

I lifted my shoulder in a short shrug.

"Well, no one wants them down her back, you know," I said.

Papa kept working. I could see this wasn't the time to convince him, so I went outside and flopped down on the wharf. I picked up my book and tried to read. The letters disappeared into the dullest recesses of my mind. The idea of a shrimping trip crowded the words out.

I thought, *There has to be some way I can talk Papa and Mama into this.*

I knew it wouldn't be easy. Even if they *could* be talked into it, even if Mr. Jake said he would go, getting Raymie to agree to taking care of his "shrimpy little sister" on his spring vacation would certainly be this side of a miracle.

The Skiff

I couldn't get that shrimping trip out of my mind. All January I kept asking about it, until Papa said I was not to mention the subject again.

I thought this was terribly unfair. Mama said we should reach high in all our dreams, no matter how wild the dreams might sound. I reminded Papa of that. He was amused. Well, his being amused wasn't amusing to me.

Just for good measure, he said, "Billy Jim's not coming down till March. No sense talking about it till he asks."

That shut me up. Besides, I could tell that being a pest was hurting my case.

Then, one Saturday late in February, Mr. Billy Jim himself showed up at our store. Raymie and I were helping Papa unload boxes when a stranger came in with Mr. Tolly. I heard Mr. Tolly introduce his friend, Billy Jim, and my ears perked right up.

"Billy Jim's looking for someone to build a skiff," Mr. Tolly said. "He's building his house right now and can't take the time to do it his-self."

Raymie was as quick as I about seizing a good opportunity. "I can build you a rowboat," he said.

Papa was so surprised his eyebrows shot into his scalp. He knew Raymie had never built a skiff. But he didn't say a word. He trusted Raymie and knew he would figure out how to get the job done.

Raymie got the job.

After the deal was made Papa and Raymie went over to Mr. Tate Dooley's lumberyard. They bought cypress timber and lots of linseed oil and paintbrushes.

Behind our house there was a rickety old barn, sort of tumbled down but safe enough. Papa had Raymie store the lumber and prepare it up there. He said that before Raymie could start building the boat he'd have to paint the lumber with linseed oil for a few weeks.

"That's so the lumber will be pliable," he explained. "You know . . . be able to bend to the shape of the skiff. When it's nice and pliable, you can start the building."

Raymie said I could help him, so every after-noon, if Papa didn't need him at the hardware shop, we'd walk up those rickety stairs of the barn to paint.

I got sick and tired of painting that lumber, but Raymie had me over a barrel. He knew about Jake and the shrimping trip, and he knew about my wanting to go. We never talked about this, but I knew he knew.

When I'd want to stop working and say I was going over to play with my friend, Jeanné, he'd say, "Well, if you don't wanna help me, that's all right. Just remember who could help *you* someday."

"That's blackmail," I said.

He laughed. "Whaddaya know about blackmail, shrimp?"

I didn't know. Not exactly.

"I know enough to know it's unfair and dishonest," I said. I made a gargoyle face at him behind his back. "And I know Brother Landry would think you're a sneaky cheat."

I could see that bothered him because he slapped his palm in the air toward me as he left and growled, "Aghh, you're nuts!"

He got his way, I thought. I took the brush out and started applying the linseed oil.

I began to smell that oil when I was asleep at night. I smelled it when I was eating grits and ham in the morning. And one Sunday night at Baptist Training Union I smelled it the entire time we sang, "Fishers of Men." When I whispered to Raymie that singing about fishermen made me smell linseed oil he started laughing and couldn't stop. When he tried he choked and couldn't sing anymore. Everyone looked at us. I was embarrassed.

When the lumber was ready to be bent into skiff shape we took the supplies down to the backyard and started building. We were proud when that little boat began to take shape. We were even more proud when we took the boat out on the bayou for a test.

Papa was so impressed he said *we* needed a new rowboat, too. He said maybe next summer, if we had enough money, we could build one for ourselves.

Easter vacation was getting close and I hadn't heard any more about Mr. Billy Jim Boisonot and his shrimp boat. I was desperate. I wasn't willing to give up my dream. I knew if that boat would be going out it would have to be the day after Easter. Easter was going to be in early April that year, and that's when we'd have time off from school.

On the first day of March I hadn't heard anything about Mr. Jake being hired by Mr. Billy Jim. I did hear that Mr. Billy Jim had moved to Bayou La Batre with his wife and baby.

Then one evening there was a knock at the door, and there he was. Mr. Billy Jim Boisonot. I stood watching as Papa answered the door. I couldn't quite make out what they were saying, although my ears were wide open.

After a short time Papa said, "Marcie, go get Mr. Jake, will you, please? And see if Raymie's in his room."

I tripled my usual lightning speed as I ran to Mr. Jake's shed out back, first making a quick stop by Raymie's room. But not until I heard Papa say, "Come on in. Helene, pet, will you get some coffee for Billy Jim?"

I yelled the message at Raymie's door, not really stopping until I got to Mr. Jake's shed out back. I stood there, watching Mr. Jake wet his comb and carefully slick his hair back. I could tell he was excited, but I was so anxious I thought he never was going to be ready.

To hurry him up, I said, "Mr. Billy Jim looked like he was in a big hurry."

Well, he probably is, I thought, excusing my fib. *He must have a million things to do, just moving in.*

We came back to the living room through the kitchen. Mr. Billy Jim was sitting on the sofa with Raymie. Mama had already set cake and coffee in front of them. I sat on the piano stool, swinging back and forth until Papa told me to stop. Well, I couldn't help it; I was nervous.

I didn't want to risk being told to leave the room, so I sat amazingly still after he scolded me. Still for me, that is; Mama's nickname for me was "Miss Jumping Catfish."

Keeping still was especially hard when they talked about the trip, but I knew better than to interrupt. And I certainly knew better than to mention the prospect of *my* going on that boat. But my brain was jumping more than my bottom; I was making plans.

Their plans were exciting to Raymie, I could tell. His eyes were shining overtime, and they looked like they were going to pop out any moment.

Mr. Billy Jim said, "Raymie, I was really impressed with the responsible and skilled way you built that skiff. That's what convinced me you'd be the right one to help Jake."

Raymie nodded his "thank you."

I was furious with Raymie. Here was the perfect time for him to talk about my part in the skiff building. But, oh, no. Not Mr. Big Shot. He didn't say one word about how I helped with that boat. Not doodly squat.

Mr. Billy Jim went on, explaining all the details to Raymie.

"Your father here tells me you have a responsible friend who'll be a great help. I'll expect you all to listen to Jake and be sure you do all the heavy throwing and lifting. You understand why I want an older, more experienced shrimper heading things up, don't you?"

"Yes, sir!" Raymie said.

I was jealous. I knew I shouldn't have been, but just because Raymie was sixteen, and a boy, he got to do all sorts of things I'd probably never get to do.

I sat there thinking, *Four would make a good crew. Raymie didn't tell him how responsible I was about the skiff. And why doesn't Mr. Jake tell him how well we get along together?*

I couldn't help what I did then. I really couldn't. I was going to explode if I didn't say something right that minute.

"Mr. Billy Jim," I blurted out, "I could go, too. I'm strong, and I'd be real good. I'll do anything Mr. Jake and . . . Hank and Raymie ask me to do." Obeying Raymie and Hank would be the hard part, but I knew I had to say it.

A terrible thing happened then. Well, terrible as far as I was concerned.

I was never as angry.

I was never as mortified.

I was never as *hurt* in my entire life.

Mr. Billy Jim laughed. That was bad enough, but then he said, "Why, what a sweet, cute thing to say, honey. Hey, when you get a little older and turn into a boy, we'll see to it you get to do just that."

The joke about my turning into a boy really exasperated me . . . as if I were stupid enough to believe things like that could happen. As if I would even *want* to be a boy. I hated it when adults joked like that.

I jumped up from the piano stool and ran from the room. A sob escaped from somewhere deep inside my wounded heart. That sob really embarrassed me; I would never want anyone to know I was crying.

I flopped on my bed and lay there, going over what Mr. Billy Jim had said and what I wished *I* had said to him.

"I like pretty dresses. I like ruffles. I like lace and pink satin. I used to like paper dolls, when I was eight. But I like crabbing, too, and swimming, and fishing, and rowing on the bayou."

Then I imagined myself looking at all of them with flashing eyes as I said what I should have said, "And I'd like shrimping, too, if y'all would just give me the chance."

I turned over and buried my head in the pillow, stifling the new set of sobs that were ready to pour out.

After a while Mama came into the room. She sat on the bed and reached over to stroke my arm in sympathy. I pulled away. That was mean, but I was embarrassed to accept her kindness.

"I know, I know," she said. "But honey, he feels terrible about it. He didn't realize. Sometimes adults don't know exactly how to be with children. They make silly jokes."

My sobs were alternating with hiccups as I said, "Well, he'd better learn fast. His little baby's gonna grow up, and I don't think she'll like that kind of silly teasing at all."

"Maybe he'll learn by then," Mama said. "Sometimes it takes a while for people to know children like to be treated in the same way adults are treated."

My hiccups dwindled down to a few sniffles. Mama just sat there. Neither of us talked for a while. She reached over to hug me. This time I didn't pull away. I liked having her on my side.

"But you know, honey," she said sweetly, "you do have to understand that it isn't very realistic to expect to go with three strong men who can handle heavy loads and know how to shrimp."

I don't know what I'd expected her to say.

"Oh, *Mama!*" I wailed.

A Change of Heart?

I sometimes felt the disappointment was too much pain for my eleven-year-old heart to bear. I tried so hard to forget that I became a nuisance around the house. I thought of all sorts of adventures and annoying plans to lessen my grief. I can see now that I wasn't being mature at all.

For instance, Raymie couldn't go swimming without my pestering him to let my best friend, Jeanné, and me go with him. If Mama happened to be going to Mobile, I made such a fuss she felt she had to take me with her. When Papa had a little time off, I insisted he take Jeanné and me crabbing around the coast.

And one day I heard he was going to Pascagoula to order supplies for his friend, Captain Wheeler, who had built a new pleasure boat. I begged so persistently to go along that he finally said, "Oh, for goodness sakes, Marcie. All right!

But when I'm buying and talking with the sales-men I don't want you asking me every minute when we're going to eat."

My one-track mind made me kind of selfish, I suppose. I felt I had been unfairly treated and deserved special attention. In a roundabout way that's how I got stuck in our new washing machine.

The way we happened to get a new washing machine was like this. There were several men in town who owned pleasure boats. That's what folks in our town called the boats that took folks fishing just for the fun of it. Some of these fish-ermen were from Mobile, and some of them were from far-off places. Once there were even some people from New York City.

I thought the pleasure boats were beautiful. They were larger, cleaner, and whiter than shrimp boats. I loved their names: *Beautiful Dreamer, Lovely Lady, Pretty Princess, Miss Lily Marie.*

When Captain Wheeler came to Papa's shop to outfit his boat I watched from my throne on the roots of the big oak. As soon as he left I ran down to the wharf to talk to Papa. He was unusually happy and swung me around, right there on the wharf. When he set me down he told me he'd made enough money to pay off some debts, donate to the church, and buy Mama a washing machine.

A washing machine! I was thrilled for Mama. Mama and Lena washed clothes by scrubbing them on washboards. Then they'd boil them in a big, black pot in our yard. When the clothes had cooled the two of them had quite a struggle to wring them out by hand without letting them touch the ground.

The new washing machine had a wringer. After the machine did the washing Mama and Lena could feed the clothes into the wringer by turning a handle. The fabric would go between two rollers that would squeeze most of the water from the clothes.

I was fascinated over this new-fangled piece of machinery. When no one was around I'd lean far into the tub and sing. I'd sing, "I've Been Working on the Railroad" with my own sad but hopeful words: "I've been working on a shrimp boat, all the livelong week."

I'd call sentences such as, "Jeanné's my best friend," or I'd make sounds like, "Oooooh, whoooo, meeeee, tooooo," just to hear the wonderful tones of those washing machine echoes.

Sometimes I'd sing "Abide with Me," "Rock of Ages," or "Stormy Weather." I'd sing until I was hoarse. Once I sang "There Is a Balm in Gilead." I wasn't much of a singer, but in that big basin of a tub my voice sounded so beautiful, the words so sad and sweet, I cried.

Well, one Saturday I was bored and maybe a little angry about the shrimp trip I was going to miss. I leaned too far into the tumbler and got stuck.

For a while I tried being nonchalant by continuing to sing, but my back began to hurt, and my legs were getting numb from being held off the floor. My stomach and ribs ached from the pressure of the steel tub rim. After a while, I was frantic. I began to pray.

Dear Lord, I begged, *please send someone in real soon, and Lord, please don't let them laugh.*

My prayers were answered. After a while I heard Mama coming in with her bag of groceries.

When she saw me, she said, "What on earth!"

"Oh, Mama," I wailed, "please get me out of here. And don't tell Papa and Raymie. And don't you dare laugh!"

It took a little doing, but by pushing one of my shoulders up, and twisting my head in a different direction, she finally got me out of that stupid machine. I was so relieved that I didn't get too annoyed when I heard Mama and Papa giggling in the living room that night.

But my side ventures and adventures didn't take my one-track mind off its obsession with the shrimping trip. My thoughts again turned to happy dreams of salt breezes fanning my face as I sat at the bow of a boat. I had visions of choppy Gulf waves. And big Gulf skies. I could almost hear the cry of seagulls swooping down in hopes of a treat.

Before Easter, when the shrimping trip was only four days away, Jeanné went home mad one day, right in the middle of a play we were planning to give on the upstairs, porchlike boards extending from the barn. Those boards made a terrific stage.

All I said was, "I wish I could go on that boat Monday morning."

Jeanné pulled that disgusted hands-on-the-hip gesture she used to show displeasure.

"You know what, Marcie," she said, "I'm sick and tired of you talking 'bout that shrimping trip. You know what you are? You're a piker shrimp, just like Hank and Raymie call you. I'm going home to play with my little sister. She can talk about something besides shrimp. Goodbye, *Shrimp!*"

She flounced off, her chin leading the way.

I felt the hurt all the way to my toes. Jeanné and I had fights sometimes, but most of the time she was willing to take up for me . . . see my side of things.

Instead of letting her know I was hurt, my feelings came out in anger.

I called after her, "Well, you can just go home, Miss Snooty Snob." I stuck my own chin out. "I don't wanna play little girlie games with you, anyhow."

After all, I thought, *I am four months older.*

Straining my voice to its loudest pitch, I added, "I'm getting too old to play with such a baby."

I really felt terrible after she left. I knew she was right. A friend can only take so much complaining about the same thing before she's had enough.

I went to the house to fix a Bread and Butter Pecan Pie. Jeanné and I had invented the recipe. We'd spread a piece of soft white Malbis' Bakery bread with gobs of butter. Next we'd carefully line every inch with big, perfect, pecan halves.

When the "pie" was finished I made a glass of iced tea and took my snack out on the back steps. I ate dejectedly. Food just doesn't taste the same when you're unhappy.

The sound of the wall telephone on the porch jangled me out of my thoughts. I placed the bread on top of the glass, put the glass on a step, and went on the porch to pick up the receiver.

"Hello," I answered.

"Marcie." It was Miss Euphonia from down at the Bayou Telephone Company. "I have a Western Union message for your mama. Will you go get her, please?"

In an important sounding voice, she added, "It's from New Orleans, Louisiana."

I took in a quick breath. "Yes, Ma'am," I said.

New Orleans, I thought. *This must be serious. That's where Aunt Lucy lives.*

I dropped the receiver and left it dangling against the wall. Mama had told me over and over that was rude of me. She said the vibrations as the receiver hit the wall probably hurt Miss Euphonia's ears. Well, too late now. I hurried to get Mama, who was out front planting zinnias.

Nervously, I told Mama she had a message from New Orleans. In haste she dropped her spade and ran up the steps to the phone.

31

When Mama heard the news she was more worried than I had ever seen her. Her oldest sister, Lucy, was ill. Aunt Lucy's daughter had sent the telegraph message. She wanted Mama to come right away; she wasn't sure whether Aunt Lucy was going to live.

I was sad for Mama and for me, too. I loved Aunt Lucy a lot. Maybe not as much as Mama did, but I felt bad. I kept thinking about how Aunt Lucy always made pralines when I visited. I remembered how she bought me Big Boy sandwiches and Snow Cones when the vendors passed her house.

My heart ached for Mama. In the next few days she cried every time she thought of Aunt Lucy, and she didn't know what to do about me. I presented a problem. There would be no school the next week, Papa would be working every day, Raymie would be shrimping with Mr. Jake, and Lena was going to Tupelo, Mississippi, to visit her family for Easter.

I loved New Orleans. Lake Ponchartrain. The colorful birds at Audubon Park. Eating beignets with café au lait at the French Quarter. But Mama didn't want me to be in New Orleans with her this time. She said she'd be going to the hospital every day . . . no time for playing or sight-seeing.

Mama was miserable.

I was miserable.

It's strange how sometimes a sad event can come right in the middle of a happy time. We had a wonderful Easter. The church was beautiful with white Easter lilies and pastel gladiolus. We sang my favorite Easter song, "Up from the Grave He Arose." I sang loudly enough to reach the church rafters. I think Brother Landry liked the way I sang; his smile was so big I thought he was about to laugh.

I wore a new, white, dotted Swiss dress. The tiny dots were red. Rows of red binding lined the ruffles. The matching hat had two ruffles lined in bias tape, too.

I scarcely ever thought I was pretty. On Easter Sunday I felt beautiful.

In the afternoon we had a party with Hank's family. But all day we felt sad and worried about Aunt Lucy. And I have to admit, I felt sad about the shrimping trip.

On Saturday Mama had called the Louisville and Nashville Railroad in Mobile and reserved her tickets for the round trip. We hadn't solved the problem of what to do about me.

At early dusk on Sunday afternoon we sat on the front porch enjoying the crocus and jonquils which had come out to celebrate Easter with us. Mama was chewing on her lips, a sure sign she was worried.

Hank's mother, Joanna, said, "Helene, maybe I can have Marcie stay with us. Hank'll be gone, you know."

Mama said, "That's just like you, Joanna, but I haven't forgotten your sister's coming from Gulfport with her family. That house of yours will

33

be busting at the seams with her four kids and your own two boys. But I sure do thank you."

Miss Joanna opened her mouth to protest, but Mama placed a hand on her arm and said, "You're always there when I need you. But don't worry, I'll think of something."

Whenever there was a surprise happening in life, Mama would say, "Why, that just came from out of the blue." I think she meant the thought came out of the sky, probably from God. Surely that's where this star-bright idea had lived before Mr. Jake reached up and brought it to our front porch on that Easter twilight.

"Miss Helene," he said, "I think I help. I know de answer, *s'il vous plait*. I have good answer, *Madame*, yes."

Mama looked at Mr. Jake with questioning eyes. She didn't seem to believe he could solve the problem. I'll have to admit, I didn't think he could, either.

She opened her mouth to say something, but he continued, his speech hesitant, his eyes sincere, and he said, "Miss Helene, *s'il vous plait* ... please ... if you let me say all de words before you speak."

He took a big breath and went on, "I take care of de young *mam'selle*."

Again, Mama started to speak, but Mr. Jake raised his hand, asking her to wait. There was so much timidity in his gesture I could see he didn't want to offend her.

"*Petite Mam'selle*, she go shrimping with us."

I actually jumped. Now *I* was ready to talk, but Mr. Jake gave me the same quieting gesture. I pressed my lips together to keep my tongue from going wild, but as he talked my heart was doing leaps and dips. Never have I had such a difficult time being silent.

But Mr. Jake didn't even look at me. His eyes met Mama's. Everyone was quiet and listened as he explained, "All de time, she be wearing lifesaver. All de time. She sleep in fo'c'sle, safe in her bunk; *M'sieu* Billy Jim have strong rail dere. Never do I let her get close to edge of boat. When we see other shrimpers, we send message to *M'sieu* Isaac. I treat like my own *jeune fille* (young girl). Dis iss promise before *le bon Dieu* (the good Lord)."

Mama and Papa were so dumbfounded they couldn't answer at the time.

I wanted to say, "Please. We don't have much time. We have to leave at three in the morning. I have to pack. Please. Please. Say something."

But I didn't. And they didn't.

Mama's hand was at her throat, and she sort of babbled, "My gracious, I . . . I don't think . . . Oh, dear . . ."

After what seemed a thousand, million, trillion seconds Papa said, "Why, that's wonderful of you, Mr. Jake. But we'll have to think about it for a while."

Think about it? Why, we have to make up our minds now! My thoughts screamed out, but this time I was wise enough to keep my tongue still.

Oh, Mama. Papa. Can't you see? This is the perfect answer!

Starting Out

After everyone was gone Mama and Papa did make up their minds. I was going to go shrimping with Mr. Jake, Raymie, and Hank!

Mama must have been ready to have a nervous fit that night. She was packing for her own journey, worrying about her sister, helping me pack, and fretting about my going out on a shrimping trip.

When she wasn't rushing about the house getting our clothes ready, she was talking to Raymie.

"Now, listen, Raymie, Mr. Jake's gonna be real busy. You're gonna have to watch Marcie every moment."

I could see Raymie wasn't at all happy about my being a part of that crew, or at the thought of watching me every moment. Well, I was a bit indignant myself to think I needed constant watching.

Raymie expelled a huge, breathy sigh and said, "Mama, have you forgotten that Hank and I are gonna be doing all the heavy stuff for Mr. Jake? We're gonna be busier than he is. I don't know how in the world this is gonna work. I really don't. I just hope she doesn't drown, that's all."

I hugged Mama and assured her I wouldn't drown.

I didn't sleep much that night. There wasn't time. At 3:00 in the morning I was out on Papa's wharf, getting ready to board Mr. Billy Jim Boisonot's boat, *Miss Pretty Pelican*, in the dark.

The sight of that long, white boat with its graceful hull sent shivers of excitement down my spine. Papa said most of these old shrimp luggers had this rounded shape. They were built by Greek shipbuilders in Pascagoula, Mississippi. Centuries ago, in Greece, their great grandfathers had built them that way, too.

Mr. Billy Jim was there to see us off. He was worried about my going. Over and over he warned Raymie. "Now, you be sure she doesn't ever go on deck without that lifesaver, you hear?"

I was so happy and excited I tried to ignore the angry feelings that welled up when he looked at me in my blue striped overalls and said, "Well! Looks like you turned into a boy after all, Mr. Marcie."

Honestly! He is so silly, I thought. I wondered if he saw me when I rolled my eyes toward heaven. Well, I didn't want to be disrespectful, but I was disgusted.

Mama came down for one last hug and to make sure my life vest was securely attached.

I had a lot of love for my mama. There was a lump in my throat as the boat moved away from our wharf, past the shacks and shops along the bayou. I'll have to admit I felt a surge of fear, a shiver of premonition that something terrible and frightening was going to happen. I closed my thoughts on that in the way you'd draw a curtain. I wanted this trip to be as wonderful as I believed it would be.

I looked back at Mama standing there, wistfully waving. I remembered too late that she was going away on a sad journey, and I had forgotten to tell her I would be praying for Aunt Lucy.

I felt better when we stopped at Breame's Ice Plant to take on a load of ice, great blocks of it.

"Why in the world do we need so much?" I wondered aloud.

Hank said, "Well, we may want a little iced tea or some cold soft drinks."

"Silly!" I said. "I know that, but what are we gonna do with this much?"

Mr. Jake shook his head at Hank. He smiled at me. "De shrimp, dey must be cold, cold or dey spoil," he said.

"And we're gonna be gone a long time—six days," Hank added.

"I knew that," I grimaced at Hank. Then I said, "Be sure to get a case of grape soda pop. That's my favorite."

All the sadness about Mama disappeared as *Miss Pretty Pelican* moved out into the bay.

The boat was bigger than we had expected. Most of the shrimp luggers in the thirties were thirty-eight or forty-five feet long, but *Miss Pretty Pelican* was fifty feet. That's because it was a freight boat that Mr. Billy Jim had bought from a shrimp canning factory in Pascagoula that had gone out of business. As a freight boat the factory owners had used it to pick up shrimp from other boats when they were out in the Gulf. That way the shrimp could be taken to the factory the day they were caught.

We were pleased the boat was big. There would be plenty of room in the hold to keep a lot of iced shrimp, and there'd be bunks for all of us. Raymie was extra happy to have the extra room because we could take Mr. Billy Jim's skiff along in case we wanted to do any exploring on the little islands we passed.

Later, as dawn broke, I sat on the bow, enjoying the feeling of the spring breezes blowing my hair back, the slight bumpiness of the boat riding the waves, the warmth of the sun promising the coming of summer.

I looked up at Mr. Jake in his pilot house. He was busy studying compasses and steering charts, but he grinned and waved at me. Hank and Raymie were coiling rope and checking the try-nets and the chains and boards on the big net.

I was happy to sit back and enjoy the ride at the bow. I wasn't certain what my duties would be, but my enjoying the ride wasn't what Raymie had in mind. We weren't out any time at all when he motioned for me to come to him. I reluctantly left my perch and stumbled over rope, cables, and anchor to reach him.

Raymie pointed at the net. "Mr. Billy Jim's try-net's kinda old. I want you to tie all these little broken cords together at the corners."

I protested, "I don't know how to do that."

"Of course you do," he said. "I've seen you tying threads on doll blankets. See? They're tied into little diamond shapes, but some of them are broken. Just tie 'em tightly at every diamond point."

I looked at the try-trawl with distaste. The net was brownish-black from oil and dirt.

"I'll get tar and oil in my fingernails," I said.

That was certainly the wrong thing to say. Raymie sighed and looked at me with an expression of such disgust I knew I'd better get to work.

"All right. *All right!*" I said as I plopped down cross-legged on the deck and pulled the net over to my side. I didn't want this oily thing ruining my new overalls.

"Put it over your lap, Empty Brain," he said, "Ain't nobody gonna have clean clothes after this week. You might as well stop trying to be Miss Meticulous Marcie."

I knew he was right, and although I cringed as I arranged the netting over my lap and began tying the greasy cords, I began to enjoy tying them and, especially, being a part of the crew.

The try-net, or try-trawl, was used for making test drags. Once we were out in the Gulf, Mr. Jake and the boys started the tests. They wanted to find the best place to shrimp . . . the place where there were the largest and best shrimp, and certainly where there were the most.

Every time they'd haul the net up they'd weigh them on a small scale. Mr. Jake would put them in small jars and have me label them. I'd have to write where the shrimp were caught and the number of shrimp in each pound. He said this would help them to know the best place to drag the master net. If there were too many in the jar, we knew the shrimp were too small and it would be against the law to catch them.

We made test drags all morning. Along with the shrimp there were all sorts of fish. They would toss the catch into a chest on the starboard side of the boat. Before I knew what it was for, I thought the chest was there to hold any treasure we might find out in the Gulf. I was glad I hadn't told anyone my thoughts, because my description didn't even come close.

The chest was about three feet deep, and after a drag I was surprised at all the different kinds of marine life there were in the try-trawl.

There were octopi, squid, eels, and every imaginable species of fish.

Raymie threw brine into the chest. I couldn't believe what happened then. All the fish and other sea creatures came to the top, and Hank and Raymie shovelled them back into the bay. The shrimp stayed in the bottom. I suppose the shrimp didn't mind the brine.

I felt bad for the fish when they frantically jumped about. They looked helpless and frightened.

"Some we keep," Mr. Jake said when he noticed my look of horror. "We have good suppers with white trout, little wan," he said.

We saved eight trout for supper that night.

I hadn't realized *I'd* be the one to clean the fish. I'd never held one of those slippery, scaly sea creatures in my hand before. I was squeamish when Hank taught me how to scale them, but when Raymie insisted I learn how to cut them open and take out the entrails and backbone, I gagged.

"I can't do it!" I wailed. "I'll throw up if I touch those nasty ole guts!"

When Mr. Jake said he would clean them for me, Raymie said, "Mr. Jake, you know I'm gonna do everything you ask me to, but I just know Mama and Papa would want Marcie to do this. She's been promising to do everything anyone on a crew would do."

Mr. Jake felt sorry for me, but he and I both knew Raymie was right. I had insisted I would be able to handle anything, and I had better prove it.

After the fish were prepared Raymie put them in the icebox.

"That's our supper, shrimp face," he said.

I thought I would never want to eat fish again. I went to the rail and immediately threw up. I didn't think anyone saw me, but later Raymie came to me, patted me on the shoulder, and said, "You did a good job, Sis. And tonight we're gonna teach you how to cook 'em, too."

I was pleased because I could see he was proud of me. I wasn't sure about the cooking part, and I certainly hadn't realized Raymie could cook. I sure was learning surprising things on this shrimping trip.

While they were taking the try-net tests I decided to make a tour of the boat. I soon realized this wasn't like any of the small craft our family had taken on pleasure jaunts. There was a pilot house, and below that, and extending almost to the end of the stern, was the cabin. The cabin was divided into several small sections. Our house in the Bayou wasn't big, but I wondered how we'd be able to live in these small spaces for six days.

The first part of the cabin, beneath the pilot's house, was the fo'c'sle where the supplies were kept. A bunk was there. I remembered that's where Mr. Jake had said I would sleep. I was glad he'd be sleeping in the pilot house above me.

Mr. Jake had told me fo'c'sle was a shortened name for forecastle. He said it was the upper deck of a boat in front of the foremast. In bigger ships the sailors slept there. There was only one bunk in my fo'c'sle.

The boys would be sleeping in bunks right off the galley. The galley was the name for the kitchen. A few short stairs went down from the galley to the engine room. Mr. Jake called those stairs the companionway. I couldn't see anything companionable about those short steps going down into that dark engine room and toilet.

There was just a curtain rigged between the toilet and the engine. I shuddered. I shuddered again when I realized something else.

"Raymie," I squealed, "Mr. Billy Jim doesn't have even one shower or tub on this boat. How're we gonna bathe?"

Raymie laughed. He took me to the back of the boat, the "aft" side as he called the stern, just behind the cabin. He showed me a big, oak barrel, lying lengthways on short wooden saw-horses behind the cabin. A black, leather flap covered almost the entire length of it. When Raymie lifted the flap, there was our water!

Indignant, I said, "Why, that's not enough water for four people to drink and bathe in for a week."

"No one ever told you shrimping would be easy, Marcie," he said, trying not to laugh again.

He showed me a dipper and a basin hanging alongside the end of the barrel.

"Better not use too much for your bath," he said. "Gotta last all week."

I shuddered again, but I tried to hide my distaste. I didn't like being dirty, but I didn't want them thinking I wasn't up to this trip. I made a real effort to hide such thoughts. I'd show them I could be a good shrimper. If I felt like complaining, I'd bite my lip. Hard.

Hank showed me the hold where the shrimp would be kept. The hold—large, square, and deep —sent shivers down my spine. The hole took up about a third of the boat, I figured. I could see it would hold a lot of shrimp and ice, but from the deck, looking down into it, the pit looked dark and foreboding. I wouldn't want to fall down there. Now there was only ice stacked on all sides.

Hank said, "We'll be chipping at that ice every time we bring a load on. We'll pack it in layers. Ice and shrimp. Ice and shrimp. By the time we get back to the bayou, the shrimp'll be colder than ice itself."

In one day Raymie, Mr. Jake, and I were beginning to turn brown. Hank was a bright, shining pink. With freckles. He was a red-head, and his skin was sensitive to the sun. He kept his hat on, even in the cabin.

I kept my lifesaving vest on in obedience to Mama, but I was getting disgusted with it. Mr. Jake wouldn't let me forget it, either. If I hadn't liked him so much I would have been irritated, but I knew he had to keep his promise.

After we ate our fried fish and potatoes we went to bed. The boys dropped the anchor out in a place on the bay where the water wasn't too deep. Mr. Jake said we'd fish in the bay since we were staying out only a week. He suggested we turn in early this first night.

"We get up early-early for de shrimp. We get up before de sun shine and den we surprise *les petit garcons.*"

I laughed to hear Mr. Jake calling the shrimp "little boys" in Cajun French.

I went to bed feeling secure and happy with Mr. Jake's pilot house above me, knowing no one could climb onto our boat, way out there in the middle of the bay. I lowered the wick on the kerosene lamp to put it out. Papa had told me to forget taking a book; there wouldn't be time to read, and we'd be too tired at night.

As the boat rocked gently, I remembered to pray especially for Mama and Aunt Lucy. Then I slipped into a sound sleep.

In the middle of the night I was awakened by the sound of footsteps in the galley behind the fo'c'sle.

That Raymie and Hank, I thought. *They can't spend more than a few hours away from food.*

I imagined them eating the cold fish, potatoes, and biscuits left over from supper. We'd put an entire fish in the little icebox. Listening to them made me hungry, too. I figured I might as well join them.

I climbed out of my bunk and padded bare-foot across the wings of the deck toward the galley. Just as I started to enter the outside hatch into the cabin section, I heard a scurrying and running, so I quickened my pace.

Those silly boys, I thought. *I don't care if they sneak a midnight snack.*

A door slammed—maybe the icebox door. I wasn't sure. But when I walked into the small galley there was no one to be seen. There was only the light of the moon, but that old moon was shining double time tonight. Through the small hatch the galley was bathed in light.

"Hank . . . Raymie," I called. "Come on out. I don't care if you're eating without me."

There was no sound at all, only the lapping of the water against the boat. I moved through the galley to the cabin where their bunks hung on the far side. They were good pretenders. Raymie was softly snoring. I returned to my bunk, a little irritated with the boys for playing tricks on me.

I woke up early the next morning when I heard Mr. Jake and the boys banging around in the galley. I wanted to be sure no one had a chance to tease me about being a baby, so I hurried to join them.

Mr. Jake had a kerosene lamp sitting on the small table. They were eating grits, biscuits, and fried ham. Raymie handed me a dish.

"You're probably not hungry after eating the leftover fish last night," Raymie said, flashing a mischievous grin at me.

"What fish?" I said. I didn't like him placing the blame on me. I knew who had enjoyed that midnight snack of cold trout.

"Aw, come on, now, Marcie," Hank said. "We know you ate the fish. Look. Nobody cares. So you got hungry. Raymie and I almost raided the icebox ourselves."

I was angry. I yelled, "You stop accusing me of doing somthing I didn't do. I'm just as honest as you. I didn't eat anything. I heard y'all in here, but, no, you had to run like little rabbits when you thought I caught you."

Mr. Jake said, "Now, you fellas, you be nice. You no tease Missy Marcie."

"You tell 'em, Mr. Jake," I said.

I saw Hank wink at Raymie. I was seething, so I took my dish of grits and fried ham out on deck. I didn't want to be around people who accused me of doing something I didn't do.

After we had eaten we were too busy to worry about who had eaten the fish. Mr. Jake directed Hank and Raymie to throw the big net over; we were going to start dragging for shrimp.

The big net was many times the size of the try-trawl and was shaped something like a funnel. There were two doorlike boards connected to chains on the wider end, and these were held by long pieces of strong manilla rope. There were corks attached to the smaller end of the "funnel."

Mr. Jake explained to me. "De boards take de net along de bottom. When de net get heavy with de shrimp, dey close to keep de shrimp in. De corks float on de top so we know where de net lie."

We caught about twenty-one hundred pounds our first day out. Mr. Jake said that would be about ten barrels. He said if we continued to catch that many on the fourth or fifth day we may need to unload some of them on another freight boat. We could see one of those big boats in the distance.

I ran short errands all day. I was beginning to love shrimping. I thought maybe I would like to own a boat someday and be the captain. The smell didn't bother me at all, once I was used to it.

Yes, the excitement, the warm sun, the laughter and joking of the boys, and Mr. Jake were all I had hoped for in those weeks when I had begged to go. The sanitary conditions weren't the best. The work was hard, the food wasn't Mama's good cooking, but I was having a thoroughly good time.

Who's There?

O n Tuesday morning I awakened early, relaxed, rested, and raring to go!

I slept like a hard-working fisherman, I thought, grinning at the idea of calling myself a man. I stretched and hopped down from my bunk, ready to start my second shrimping day.

A clink in the galley made me think the boys were up, already starting breakfast. I decided to join them and padded over to the galley. I was surprised to see no one was there.

A kerosene lamp in the boys' cabin sent a slanting ray of light through a crack in the door and onto the table, spotlighting an empty bowl. Curious, I picked the bowl up. A few grains of grits were left, but it had been scraped almost clean.

I could hear Raymie and Hank talking in their cabin as they dressed. I knew they hadn't come into the galley yet. I decided not to mention the bowl, but I had an eerie feeling. Something strange was happening on our boat.

When we had finished breakfast and started the necessary chores I stopped for a moment to really *look* at the beautiful day. The sky was a deeper blue than I had ever seen in Bayou La Batre. The waters reflected the blue, too.

We continued to catch shrimp. I was trying to be the best worker I could be. I lifted loads with the boys, cleaned fish, helped scrub the decks. I desperately wanted to keep up with Hank and Raymie. I had never realized I could work and enjoy it.

I couldn't wait to get back home to show Mama how I had learned to gut a fish, and now I knew how to cook them for supper. I planned to surprise her one day when she got home from a church or PTA meeting by having a fish dinner cooked, complete with a shrimp cocktail in hot sauce, with fried potatoes and biscuits.

I was dirtier than I'd ever been, certainly more sun-browned, and I knew I had never been this tired. Or as proud.

Wednesday night we had a party with other shrimpers. I'm sure that doesn't seem possible if a person has never been out on a shrimp boat. I had never heard of such an event. But we did have a party!

On Monday and Tuesday we had seen other shrimp boats dotting the horizon. We'd hit a good spot for dragging, and the other shrimpers evidently had, too.

On Wednesday we had another good haul. When Hank and Raymie pulled the trawl up for the last drag of the day, the net was filled with shrimp. Mr. Jake put me to work chipping ice while the boys separated the unwanted sea creatures and iced the shrimp in the hold.

When we were finally done for the day, we trooped over to the oak barrel to wash up. Just then another boat, *Camellia Ann*, dropped anchor next to us.

We all looked up curiously. The captain called out, "Wanna share supper? We got some mighty tasty red beans and rice over here stewing up."

Mr. Jake was full of smiles. "Yah. We love to pass pleasure with you. What we got to share, boys?"

Raymie was quick to say, "Jambalaya. In the icebox."

"We got plenty, plenty?" Mr. Jake asked Raymie.

Raymie laughed and answered in the Cajun way, "Plenty, plenty."

"Come on board!" Hank yelled.

That's how the party got started. It just sort of grew and widened from there. Before we knew how it happened, Mr. Hirus Landau and his crew had dropped anchor, too. Their contribution was a pot of turnip greens and a skillet of corn bread.

I felt kind of shy around all these men. They were surprised to see me, but they were polite and respectful. Most of them traded with Papa and Raymie, and I knew some of them from our church.

There were a lot of teasing remarks. They wanted to know how on earth Mr. Jake had talked my parents into letting their little "oyster pearl" go out on a boat.

I was getting tired of their teasing. When I looked up and saw *The Lillie Mae* come alongside, I was gladder than anything to see my friend, Pierre Delacruz. I didn't know he had come out with his dad and brother. I was ready to dance the light fantastic. I'd never known exactly what the light fantastic was, but I was ready to dance it.

Mr. Jake was "happy, happy" to see Mr. Delacruz, Pierre's father. Mr. Delacruz had lived in Louisiana, too. He and Mr. Jake had a lot in common. Especially food. Mr. Delacruz had cooked up a pot of court bouillon—a wonderful mixture of tomatoes, potatoes, fish, garlic, rice, and spices.

Mr. Jake and Mr. Delacruz addressed one another as *"M'sieu."*

"*M'sieu* Luis, dis de best court bouillon I had since I live in Houma," Mr. Jake said, slapping Mr. Delacruz on the back soundly in the way men do when they like one another.

Pierre wasn't as friendly as usual. At first he acted as if he didn't even know who I was. I think he was afraid the men would start teasing him and say he had a girlfriend.

Well, I didn't care if they did tease. I was more than pleased to see someone closer to my age, someone I *knew*. I took the situation in hand by opening two bottles of grape soda and taking them to where he sat on the bow.

I knew how to get Pierre's attention. Grape soda helped, but the "*piece de resistance*" as my mama often said (meaning the thing a person can't resist) was when I told him about our strange "ghost."

"Aww, Marcie," he said, making a face, "we already found we were wrong about Miss Tilly being a witch. Like your mama says, you have a mighty powerful imagination."

That irritated me. Mama had often accused both Pierre *and* me of having wild imaginations. I told him. "Your imagination's worse than mine," I said, glaring at him. "At least I always tell the truth."

"Well, I'm older than you," he said smugly. "I'm outgrowing that kind of stuff."

Now I was determined to get him interested. He wasn't going to "out mature" me.

"Well, think of it this way," I said, defending my story, "there's no place to hide on a boat. We're out in the middle of the bay away from every other boat. And I even went in to look at Raymie and Hank after I found the bowl, and they were both sound asleep."

I could tell he was getting hooked on my story, but just like one of those fish that wiggle and turn when caught, he became unhooked. He laughed. From that moment I was determined to

solve the mystery of the disappearing food—just to show him.

Even so, I enjoyed having Pierre there, and sharing supper was a lot of fun. The men laughed, and joked, and told wild tales of their fishing and shrimping exploits.

Jolly Joisant hopped over to his boat and came back with a fiddle, and soon the boat was rocking with music. Eddie Rodin started dancing a jig and almost fell into the hold with the shrimp and ice. Hank just caught him in time. We laughed harder than the incident was funny. I think that was because the day had started for everyone before the sun came up, the work had been steady and hard, the sun was hot, and now we were relaxed and our stomachs were full.

Everything seemed sharp and clear that night, as if the angels had been out polishing the world. The water glowed with sudden flashes of phosphorus. The moon and stars glimmered and gleamed. And surely the tones of the fiddle were as beautiful as anything I'd ever heard on the radio. I think something about the water made the music better.

One by one the shrimpers went back to their boats. Mr. Luis and Mr. Jake talked for a while, nostalgically lapsing into their native Cajun French.

The Delacruzes were the last to leave. As their boat hoisted anchor and chugged away, I heard Pierre yelling something to me.

"What'd he say?" I asked the boys.

"He told you to take care of your ghost." Hank laughed.

Raymie laughed, too. I might have laughed back, but I was furious. But my anger just made it worse, sending them into unnecessary spasms of crazy laughter.

Fiddler Crabs

Often, when I'd had an especially good or bad day, I'd have what my mama called "a serious case of insomnia," like it was some disease or something. Well, sometimes it could seem as bad as a disease. I'd lie there, all excited, or worried, or full of plans for the next good time, or how I was going to get out of some predicament. The night after that wonderful party on our shrimp lugger I had a triple quadruple case of insomnia.

I tossed. I turned. I sighed. I tried to stop thinking. I tried to think of black velvet. Someone had told me that could make you sleepy. I tried boring myself to sleep by going over my multiplication tables. But nothing worked. I could tell the way the moon had moved across the sky that it was really late . . . maybe the middle of the night.

The bay was calm. I could hear a soft lapping of water against the boat. Such a peaceful sound should have made me sleepy. But then I heard someone on deck.

I sat up in the bunk, straining my ears to hear.

Why, there's someone softly singing. I'm certain of it.

I hopped down from the bunk, stubbing my toe on a box. "Ouch!" I said, then put a hand over my mouth, furious with myself. Whoever was out on deck would surely have heard and disappear by the time I got out there.

I scurried to deckside as quickly as I could. Once on deck I stood, silent as the air itself, listening. Distinctly there was the sound of a strange in-and-out hissing. I turned to run back to my cabin in terror when I realized the sound was my own scared breathing. I expelled a long, frightened breath and, trembling, I began to circle the deck.

There was something crawling on the floorboards. I leaped in fear when I almost stepped on it. To be certain no one was behind me I looked about before I stooped to examine.

Fiddler crabs! There were fiddler crabs crawling about on the decking. Fascinated at finding them on shipboard I walked about, looking for more. There must have been twenty-five or thirty of them, maybe more. They were scurrying about with frantic movements of pincers and claws.

Jeanné and I liked to play with fiddler crabs. They are just itty-bitty crabs, not much longer than an inch, but they have a large pincer for fighting. We loved to pick them up. They'd wave their claws frantically and try to snap at us with their big pincer. Mama told us they were called fiddler crabs because they move their large pincer back and forth the way a person does when playing a violin, or fiddle.

But the mysterious thing was, fiddler crabs didn't ever show up on boats. In fact, a fiddler crab couldn't even get *on* a boat. The boat would have to be close to the sand or marsh, and, even then, fiddler crabs don't care for unprotected spaces like the side of a boat. They are forever scrambling in and out of their sand or mud holes.

These crabs had to have been *carried on.* And I could bet who did it—Hank and Raymie.

I went to the galley to find a sack for the crabs. While I was looking for the sack, I heard footsteps again. I hurried up to the deck, closing the hatch with a bang. If the boys were playing a trick they'd be certain to hide now. On deck I looked about, but no one was there.

I couldn't understand how anyone could have possibly gotten on deck and hidden that quickly. A ghost, maybe? I shuddered. I consoled myself by remembering how Mama had told me, repeatedly, to "stop that silly ghost talk."

I gathered the remaining crabs, all those I could find, and took them to the fo'c'sle. I punched holes in the brown paper bag, tied the top with a string, and crawled back into my bunk. When I couldn't sleep, and I knew morning was near, I went to the galley and started breakfast.

I made the coffee, smiling as I thought of how I'd surprise Mama when I made coffee for her at home. I started the water boiling for grits, and I fried slices of ham.

Thoughts of home and showing off my new cooking skills didn't stay with me long. I kept wondering about the crabs. It just didn't seem like the sort of practical joke either Raymie or Hank would pull on me. They certainly knew I wasn't afraid of fiddler crabs. They weren't slimy like shrimp. That's why I hadn't liked touching shrimp.

"Hey, Shrimp," Hank said as he entered the galley. "You getting to be a real A-plus helper around here, aren't you? Maybe Raymie and I'll let you join our Big Boys Club some day. That is, if we ever organize one."

"You know something, Hank," I said, "I can't for the life of me figure why you and that stupid brain brother of mine would think, even for a moment, that *I'd* think that fiddler trick was cute."

Hank looked at me as if I had lost my mind.

"Have you lost your marbles?" he asked, staring at me with obvious disgust.

"No!" I shot back. "But it looks like that silly big brother of mine, and probably you, too, have lost all *your* marbles."

Raymie and Mr. Jake came up about then and Raymie asked, "What are you in such a steam about, Marcie?"

63

I was frustrated and feeling both doubtful and foolish, so I yelled, "Those stupid fiddler crabs! Why in the world would you try to scare me with *fiddler crabs*? If you think I'm afraid of a few little harmless fiddler crabs, well . . . well, you've lost all your marbles, Raymond Anderson Delchamps."

Hank lifted his hands in a gesture of ignorance and said, "Could you maybe just show us what you're talking about, Marcie?"

I shrugged and left the galley in a huff. I was beginning to think they were sincere and really didn't know what I was talking about. But they'd been able to fool me before. I raced to my bunk to get the sack full of fiddler crabs.

They were gone. Gone. Nowhere to be seen. Why, this was impossible. I was perplexed. I was embarrassed. How could I prove I'd had them if they couldn't be found?

I went back to the galley and feebly tried to confirm the existence of the crabs. I was beginning to believe maybe I *had* lost my marbles.

The boys laughed at me until Mr. Jake said, "Iss enough joke, Raymie. Hank. Missy Marcie feel bad. Stop, *s'il vous plait.*"

"Okay," Raymie said, but he couldn't help adding, under his breath, "I didn't think you still played with itsy-bitsy baby doll fiddler crabs, little sister."

I took my plate to a place in the wings and ate in silence, seething.

Something about their responses bothered me. They really didn't act as if they had brought them on board. I could spot their teasing most of the time. Raymie would usually try to hide a smile by twisting his lips in a telltale way. Hank would turn his head away to keep me from hearing a snort of choked laughter.

But if they hadn't brought those crabs on board, who had?

Another Member
of the Crew

Thursday we had another hard-working, satis-factory day. I was proud to be actually work-ing on a shrimp boat. I couldn't wait to get back home and tell all my friends about my adven-tures—even about the "ghost."

I suppose Raymie and Hank couldn't help teasing me about the ghost. On this trip they had been far more respectful of me than they ever had been back on dry land. But my imagi-nation had always been something for my entire family to tease me about, so I shouldn't have expected Raymie to stop now. It did irritate me that Hank felt he had the same right.

That night I lay in bed, remembering the odd happenings of the last few nights. Where in the world had those fiddler crabs come from? No answer came, so I decided to forget about them.

I didn't mind anymore that my sheets were no longer clean. I stretched and sighed with contentment. I said my prayers, thanking God for everything, even the clean sheets at home. I asked him to care for Mama, and Papa, and Aunt Lucy.

Then I slept. I don't believe I had ever slept as soundly as I did that night, or since. But early in the morning, before daylight, when there was only a slight glow of yellow and pink in the eastern sky and the bay waters were a calm and steely grey, I heard a noise in the galley again.

My first thought was, *Aha! I've caught them*, but then I figured Mr. Jake had gotten up just a little earlier to start breakfast. I decided to get up and help. I walked the short distance down the companionway to the galley.

I can't begin to express the feelings I had when I saw a little boy eating at the table. We both jumped when we saw one another. He made an attempt at moving away, but I reached out and grabbed him.

He was a little black boy, about four years old, not as dark as our cook, Lena. He was the color of a pecan shell. His hair was short around his head, black and curly-tight. His eyes were large and the color of a cup of coffee with a little cream poured in. In each cheek there was a deep dimple.

His beauty struck me the moment I saw him, but all other thoughts were blocked at the realization that here was my "ghost."

He was terribly afraid.

"No! No, no," he cried. "Please." He began to whimper as he struggled to escape my grasp. I held on tightly. This was my proof of truth. There was no way I was going to let my "ghost" go.

"Shhh," I cautioned. I gently covered his mouth and motioned for him to come with me. I led him back to my fo'c'sle quarters. When his crying continued my heart hurt for him. He was so young. So little.

I sat by the hatch so he couldn't get away. He backed against the boxes of supplies, trying not to cry. I felt sorry for him.

"Don't cry," I said.

On my knees I went toward him, but he jumped in fear and moved away.

Oh, the poor little fellow, I thought. *Why, he's scared to death of me.*

"There, there," I crooned. "No, no, no . . . please don't be afraid of me. I won't hurt you. Honest."

I put my arms around him and hugged. He melted into my hug. I was surprised, then, to find I was crying, too.

From the galley below I could hear someone beginning to prepare breakfast.

Again, I said, "Sshh, shh," hoping to keep him quiet until I had some explanation to give the others, but I could hear Raymie, coming up the four steps to the fo'c'sle, and saying, "Marcie, I know you've already eaten, but why in the world didn't you start breakfast for everyone else?"

He'd seen the empty bowl and had come to tease.

There was no time nor place to hide the boy, and I can tell you I have never seen such an expression of surprise and bewilderment on anyone's face as Raymie's when he looked into the fo'c'sle hatch. He stared in disbelief as he saw me and that little boy tightly holding on to one another, with tears running down both our faces.

"What in the world?" he gasped.

I whispered, "He . . . he's our ghost."

Raymie immediately saw how afraid the little fellow was. He squatted down and said softly, "Aw, don't be afraid. No one's gonna hurt you."

Just then Mr. Jake and Hank appeared. The amazement on their faces was more than my dramatic imagination had hoped for.

The space in the fo'c'sle was too small for all of us and we were soon on deck. All five of us.

The boy stood, shyly staring at these tall fellows, his eyes great, round, circles of fear, his lips trembling. He sidled up to me and slipped his hand into mine. We were quickly becoming friends. "Soul mates" is what Mama called it when people shared loving feelings and kind of "hooked on" to how another person felt.

"You got name?" Mr. Jake kindly asked him.

"Lissez," the boy said. "Lissez Jamison." He held up four fingers and added, "I'm four."

Lissez had the soft, rounded accents of his people. Of course, we had the accents of our people, too, but we didn't know that. When Northerners came to Bayou La Batre on fishing trips they'd tell us how "charming" we sounded. We thought *they* had the accents, just the way we thought the black people who lived up the highway from us sounded different to us. Later, I realized we sounded similar.

Mr. Jake said, "Lissez *'ti* name?"

The boy didn't answer. I was sure he'd never heard Cajun dialect. I knew *'ti* was a contraction for the French word *petit*. I'd heard Mr. Jake use that expression often.

"He means nickname," I explained.

"Name Ulysses Jamison," the boy said. "Nickname, Lissez."

"Glad for to meet you," Mr. Jake politely said. "Where you hide?"

Lissez solemnly looked at Mr. Jake, then beckoned with his finger. He led us down the short companionway to the engine room. A small bench was there. He pointed to it, but we didn't understand. Then, placing his hands on the top of the bench, the part against the wall, he lifted it.

This was not a bench, after all. This was a chest, with a top attached with hinges. The chest was empty except for a thin, rumpled blanket.

Dismayed, Mr. Jake lapsed into Cajun French, "*Mais, non. Non, non, le petit garcon* no sleep in box?"

Raymie said, "Why, I sit here every morning when I put my boots on."

71

Each of us remembered times we had sat on the chest or used it for something. We were dumbfounded.

"*Le pauvre garcon*," Mr. Jake said, shaking his head in sympathy. "How he stand de heat, de smell of gas from de engine room? He little, little. De space little, little."

The boy began to cry again. He was afraid of what we were going to do to him. I knelt beside him and placed my hands on his narrow shoulders.

"Lissez, we're not gonna hurt you. We like you. We're gonna help you," I said.

My "soul mate" clung to me.

"I a good little boy," he said, earnestly.

"Aww, listen, y'all, isn't he darling?" I cried out.

Everyone smiled. I could tell they agreed.

Mr. Jake asked him, "Iss hungry, *n'est ce pas*?"

Lissez didn't understand. He stared at Mr. Jake with those solemn eyes.

"Are you hungry, little fella?" Hank asked.

Lissez actually grinned. "No, Sir," he said.

We all laughed, remembering the empty bowl on the galley table.

I had a sudden thought. I had to know.

"Lissez," I asked, "Did you maybe bring a bag of fiddler crabs on board?"

He answered with a broad smile, "Yes'm, I collected lots of 'em before I got on de boat."

Triumphant, I turned to the others. "There! You see? I'm not crazy!"

I looked at Lissez again. "Why'd you bring 'em, honey?"

He looked down at the deck with shyness. "To play with 'em while I was going to foreign lands."

"Of course," I said. Of course a little boy would want something to play with on a trip.

We wondered at the "foreign lands" bit, but other questions didn't bring forth any clarifying answers. When we realized we weren't getting anywhere finding out about our stowaway, Mr. Jake suggested the boys head for the galley. He was going to the pilot house to chart our course for the day while they cooked. I was given "time off" for the time being. He gave me the happy job of caring for our new little friend.

"You find de truth about *le petit garcon*," Mr. Jake said. "You give story when we eat, hah?"

The Truth

This was the most beautiful day I had seen since we had been out. We had slipped around Bird Island and gone into the Gulf for better shrimping. Looking at the full, white clouds I remembered this was still Easter week. The soft, moist breezes of spring made the days cool, even as the warmth of the spring sun browned us. The April sun came as gently as the April breezes.

I took Lissez to my favorite place in the bow. The Gulf was calm this morning. We had cast anchor at a buoy, and the water lapped at our rounded, white hull.

Mr. Jake had insisted Lissez wear a life jacket, and the two of us sat in the bow, huddled together as closely as our life vests permitted.

"Now, Lissez," I said, "I think you need to tell us everything about how come you're on this boat. Ain't nobody gonna hurt you, ain't nobody gonna be mad at you, but it's only fair you tell us so we can help."

"Yes'm," he said.

"That's the second time you called me ma'am. Don't call me ma'am," I protested. "I'm only eleven."

"Yes'm," he said, and then he realized he'd done it again, and we both giggled.

His story was heartbreaking. I was saddened as he talked.

Ever so often, in my silent thoughts, I'd say a prayer. "Please, dear Lord, help us to know how to help my darling little Lissez."

I was already thinking of him as "my." *My* little friend. *My* little brother. *My* darling little Lissez.

He said his mama had died when he was born, and he'd been living with his papa. But last month his papa had disappeared when he was looking for work over in St. Louis. No one had heard from him or been able to find him. Lissez had run away from the woman who was caring for him. The neighbors had called the welfare office in Mobile. Lissez was going to have to live in an orphanage.

"I don't wanna live in a orphanage," he said, his eyes filling with tears again. "I wants my papa. My papa good to me. My papa play ball with me in the field by our house. I don't know what gonna happen to me. I think he dead."

"Oh, no, he's probably not dead," I said, but I wasn't sure I meant it. If the neighbors had already been trying to find him and they hadn't had any luck . . .

"How'd you get to Bayou La Batre?" I asked. I figured Dixon's Corner, where the black folks lived, must be about twelve miles from Bayou La Batre.

He lowered his head and looked up at me shyly.

"I come in Miss Lena's husband's truck when he come to work at the shrimp factory."

I gasped. "Lena? You know Lena? She's our friend. Did she know you were there?"

"Nah," Lissez said, shaking his head solemnly. "She don't know. Mistuh Handley don't know, either. I hide in the back."

"But what were you planning to do, Lissez?" I asked. I reminded myself that he was only four. I suppose he'd thought he'd do anything to keep from going to that orphanage.

"I was gonna git on a ship and go to some foreign land across the ocean where they don't have no orphanage. Could you all take me there?"

Poor little boy. He couldn't know these fishing and shrimping boats often went into the Gulf of Mexico, but they didn't land in foreign ports. They just fished and shrimped and fished. Also, he didn't realize other countries had orphanages, too.

"Will Mr. Jake take me back to the welfare lady?" he wailed when I explained this.

"I don't know, Lissez. But Mr. Jake's a good man. And my mama and papa's good folks. And,

Brother Landry, over at our church, he's good folks, too."

Lissez squealed and said, "I knows Brother Landry. He comed to our church and sat by the altar with Brother William when our choir sang for your church."

I remembered. I had been there, too. A small group from our church had gone to sing and to hear their choir sing. We'd brought angel food and devil's food cakes and cornbread. The folks at Dixon's Corner had made the best ribs and turnip greens I had ever tasted.

I wondered how I could have gone to a service at the First Baptist Church of Dixon's Corner and not remembered seeing this beautiful little boy.

Hank, Raymie, and Mr. Jake shrimped all day, and they brought in an especially big haul. Lissez helped me chip the ice for the hold. He was good help in the kitchen, too. But at four years of age he was too young to forget his missing papa. Ever so often he'd moan, or whimper. His pitiful little sounds made me hurt all over.

I was anxious to report my findings to Raymie and the others as soon as supper was over.

There was a second bunk in the pilot house, and Mr. Jake and I put Lissez to bed there after supper. I told him a story, and Mr. Jake and I both did our best to assure him we'd get help for him and try to find his daddy.

Lissez was asleep before we had blown out the wick on the coal oil lamp.

As tired as they were, all three of the fellows were anxious to hear about Lissez. When I told them, I had a hard time not crying, but I forgot my usual dramatics. This tragic happening didn't need any added drama.

When I'd finished, Raymie said, "What do you think we can do, Mr. Jake? Should we send a message by someone returning to the Bayou? Have someone meet us? Let 'em know he's okay?"

"Oh, please, don't," I cried. "I know we have to tell someone as soon as we get there on Saturday, but it's just one day . . . Look. Papa and Mama'll do something. I think they know a judge who could be of some help."

"Maybe his daddy ain't dead," Hank suggested.

"Maybe," I said, "but if he really loves Lissez, he's not gonna stay away without getting in touch with him."

"That's why I think he's dead," Raymie said.

"If we no find papa," Mr. Jake offered, "I take him. He live with me in shed."

That was just like Mr. Jake.

"That would be really terrific!" I said, warming to this great idea. Lissez could be my little brother.

"A lot of folks wouldn't like it, a nigra living at your house," Hank reminded us.

"Not my mama," I said. "My mama says everybody's the same in God's eyes, and that means they gotta be the same in our eyes, too."

78

"Yeah, Miss Helene really practices what she preaches," Hank said, shaking his head in admiration.

Raymie brought us back to reality. "It won't be that easy," he said. "There's sure to be legal problems. You just can't adopt someone without going through the law."

Even so, we all began to have happy feelings about the possibilities. In the rosy glow of love we let ourselves forget the problems.

The Squall

All four of us were happy about our big haul. Raymie and Hank were already counting the money they'd make. I began to figure how much I might possibly be able to put in my piggy bank, too.

We were caught up in a sort of spring fever. The late afternoon Gulf was more calm than we had experienced on our entire trip, even calmer than the bay yesterday. There weren't any flowers out here to remind us of spring, but there was a spring freshness in the air. The beauty of the morning had turned into an even more beautiful evening. The moon made a glimmering lane across the waters.

Mr. Jake lifted his arms to the sky in a gesture of happiness to the moon. "*Le nuit, tres joli. Bon,*" he said.

We knew enough French to know he was saying the night was pretty, and that it was very good.

We felt it, too. We had experienced a warming love in our meeting with a little boy. We'd had a good haul. Our supper had been lip-smacking good. Mr. Jake had cut our leftover grits into rectangles, fried them, and made ham gravy. We'd had a pot of tasty lima beans with salt pork and finished off the last of our watermelons.

We cast anchor right there in the middle of the Gulf. The water wasn't too deep at this point. We decided we wouldn't start the engines again to find a better spot to anchor. We sat in the dark on deck for a long time.

"Never have I see Gulf so quiet, quiet," Mr. Jake said.

We talked of many things, especially Lissez. We made plans we knew were only dreams, but we were caught in a trawl-net of love which made unlikely dreams seem possible.

We talked about God and how and why we knew him.

Mr. Jake said, "I know for sure about de *bon dieu*; *M'sieu* Isaac, *Madame* Helene, they show what they do."

Raymie and I looked at each other and shared a moment of pride for our good parents.

The boys told tales of daring pranks they'd played on friends in Bayou La Batre. Mama would have wanted to die right then if she had known.

Mr. Jake talked of carefree days as a boy in Louisiana, first on Bayou La Fourche and, later, as a hard-working young man in Houma. He told of his wife who had died.

We smiled as we remembered how, just a short while ago, we had been afraid of "old" Jake. We'd thought he was a ghost. We laughed long and loudly at that thought. Our dear, gentle friend . . . a ghost? How could we have ever been so foolish as to think that?

I didn't talk much about my life. I hadn't lived as long as they had, and I was afraid they wouldn't be interested in the games Jeanné and I played.

But on this night I had no need to be the center of attention. I was proud to be a part of the crew. I was proud to have Raymie as my brother. I loved Mr. Jake. I was even willing to admit I loved Hank, too, even though his teasing sometimes hurt.

None of us wanted this time of warm companionship to end, but eventually we gave in. Our bodies were tired. There would be lots of work Saturday morning to get one last haul before we headed home.

After sleepy, relaxed "goodnights" we called it a day and went our various ways to crawl into our bunks. The first few evenings out I had heard Raymie and Hank talking for a long time. Tonight they were silent. They must have fallen asleep immediately.

I snuggled into my bunk. I made up my mind I would lie there for a while and make happy plans for a future with Lissez. Instead, the enchanted spring night wrapped itself around me, a snug, warm quilt of contentment. In a moment I was asleep and having contented dreams.

Those blissful dreams became a terrible nightmare. I awakened to the dread understanding that I wasn't asleep. I was being tossed, and thrown, and pulled about by some terrible force of nature. I began to realize we were in the midst of a Gulf storm, and *Miss Pretty Pelican* was in its powerful hands.

As I made an effort to climb out of my bunk and go on deck, I heard Mr. Jake's voice, barking commands to Raymie and Hank.

"Hoist anchor! Hoist anchor!"

I stumbled out to the deck. Raymie and Hank hadn't had time to put on work boots or slickers or shirts. They were in their work pants, their bodies wet from a driving rain and the waves that splashed across the decks.

Hank was tugging on the cover of the hold, tightening it, trying to save our shrimp catch. Raymie was lying across the bow, most of his body hanging out of the boat, straining with all the strength he had to lift our two-hundred-and-fifty-pound anchor. I dropped to the deck beside him and grappled with the rope, too.

The wind had the boat standing on its bow one moment and on its aft the next. As Raymie and I tugged together, a giant wave washed over us. My heart leaped as Raymie slipped. I grabbed

his arm and held on with all my might. Together we managed to get him back on the aft boards of the deck again without his losing his grip on the anchor ropes.

Raymie hoarsely cried out, "Now, Marcie!" Together we pulled as hard as we could. With a huge clatter, the anchor landed on deck. We fell back, breathing hard.

The winds pushed us so hard we could barely stand on two feet. I saw Mr. Jake, stumbling along the cabin wall, grasping at anything he could find to keep his balance.

He cried out to us, "We go bay side. Bird Island!"

Behind Jake I saw Lissez staggering out of the pilot house. At that moment Raymie and Jake saw him, too.

Mr. Jake, Raymie, and I all screamed, "No! Lissez, *no!*"

But the boy was frantic with fear. He scrambled down the companionway. Mr. Jake, closest to him, ran towards him with outstretched arms.

At that moment a wave swept across the deck and rolled over the cabin. As Raymie and I gained balance by holding tightly to the structure of the fo'c'sle we watched in paralyzed terror as we saw Mr. Jake, holding Lissez in his arms, being washed into the roiling waters of the Gulf.

As this horrible scene met my eyes a memory flashed through my mind of childish fears I had known in the past. These fears had been unreal:

ghosts, witches, and other strange creatures. In this half-moment I knew *this* fear was real.

"Oh, dear God," I prayed, "please don't let 'em drown."

In the pilot house Hank turned on the powerful electric searchlights. He scanned the waters, swivelling the beam so that it reached both sides and behind us.

Something was being tossed about in the waters below. Our hearts leaped in hope, but the dark form in the water was Mr. Billy Jim's empty rowboat, the boat Raymie and I had made. The skiff had been washed overboard, too.

Mr. Jake and Lissez were nowhere in sight.

Hank went up to the pilot house in an attempt at controlling *The Pretty Pelican*. The boat was leaping and falling with the force of the storm. Raymie and I rushed about, leaning from both port and starboard sides, calling, "Mr. Jake! Lissez!" until our voices were hoarse. The thunderous noise of the wind drowned our shouts, but hope kept us trying.

There were no answering cries.

I was pleading, "Oh, please, God. No. No. Don't let 'em drown. Please. Please."

Hank started the engine. In hopeless despair Raymie and I gave up. We fought the raging winds to get to the pilot house. Hank and Raymie took turns piloting. If we were going to save ourselves we knew we had no other choice but to head for Bird Island as quickly as possible.

Heartsore, we headed towards the bay and the island to seek the protection of the trees and sand dunes there.

Miss Pretty Pelican was tossed about as if she were a paper boat in a bathtub, blown by a little child. We held on to each other, the wheel, the bunks, anything to keep from falling.

As we rounded the tip of Bird Island the wind slowly stopped its frenzied howling and forceful fury. The intense rain continued to fall. We were not yet able to see the waters around us.

Eventually the rain stopped. We anchored in a small cove off the island. We stood at the windows of the pilot house, praying for some sign of hope. None came. Never have there been three more dejected, heartbroken people. I wanted to sob, scream, shriek with grief and horror, but I couldn't.

Raymie kept blaming himself. Then Hank took the blame. I felt guilty, too.

"I think I saw Lissez first," I said. "I should have run to get him that very moment."

"You couldn't have, Honey," Raymie said, hugging me with one arm and stroking my wet bangs with the other. "Why, you were helping me with the anchor, and if you hadn't helped me, *I* would have drowned. I don't know where you got the strength, but I couldn't have done it without you."

We both knew the strength had come from a Power more able than we. I could sense his sincerity in saying nice things to me. I loved having my usually gruff brother showing me love and tenderness, but a compliment couldn't heal the hurt I was feeling.

We looked through the telescope, trying to find some sign of our friends. Finally, we gave up and scanned the horizon in search of other shrimp boats. Maybe we could find some of our friends of the night before. But we saw no one. We seemed to be alone in a hostile sea.

"What are we gonna do?" I looked up at Raymie as I might have looked toward Papa if he were there. There had to be someone to make the decisions.

Raymie's voice broke when he said, "Oh, Marcie, I don't know. I don't know."

Wet and miserable, we huddled in the pilot house and stared out at the water. No one suggested going to bed. We didn't want to be alone.

Early Saturday morning the sun came out, a brilliant light, so sharp we were unable to look at its brightness. The bay was a deep, grey satin, studded with diamond sunbeams, but this beauty gave us no happiness today. A brisk, cool breeze was blowing. The squall had brought a change of weather.

"How could a storm have come up so quickly?" I wondered aloud.

"I dunno," Raymie answered.

"I've heard spring squalls do that sometimes," Hank mused.

We stood on deck now, jackets pulled on against the cold, looking out at the calm sea, our eyes searching the shoreline for a dread glimpse of the skiff or washed-up bodies.

I made the decision.

"Raymie, I think we should get back to the bayou right now. We need to tell everyone what happened, and although it isn't important now, I guess it's our responsibility to get Mr. Billy Jim's shrimp over to the factory."

"Yeah, I think you're right." He stroked my head again. He clapped an arm around Hank's shoulder and in a hoarse voice, strained with held-back tears, he said, "Agree, ole buddy?"

"Yep," Hank said.

I put a hand on Raymie's arm.

"Wait," I said. "There's something we have to do first."

I started saying the Twenty-third Psalm, looking out at the water. Raymie and Hank said the words with me.

"Let's all say a silent prayer for Mr. Jake and Lissez," Raymie said.

We were quiet then. The only sounds were the pleasant *pullip, pullip* of water lapping on the hull, a light wind blowing through the mast, and the call of a gull.

"Amen," Raymie said, and Hank and I joined in.

Raymie started the engines. We were silent, each looking out at the sky and water, thinking our own thoughts, saying our own prayers.

Home

In a daze the three of us went about the chores of piloting, washing the decks, cleaning the galley, making certain the shrimp were iced, coiling the ropes, and folding the nets. We felt a heightened sense of responsibility . . . to Mr. Jake, to Mr. Billy Jim, to our folks, to ourselves. The world had turned upside down for us, but we wanted to do something to make it a little bit right again.

And, too, the busywork kept us from breaking. We didn't mention Mr. Jake or Lissez. We talked of how many pounds of shrimp we had caught, and what we should do as soon as we reached the bayou.

The first sight of the bayou filled me with hope. The first few shacks, the boats being repaired on shore, the marsh grass, dark green and lush against the blue skies, all spoke of home and help.

We went straight to Dolittle's Shrimp Factory to unload the shrimp. We were surprised we'd caught so many in only four days. The workers at the factory were, too, but we had to tell them the terrible news first. Everyone was sick with horror. They had heard of the storm. Some of the other shrimpers had come in. The factory workers had heard how suddenly and powerfully the storm had come up.

There was no news of Mr. Jake or Lissez.

Raymie went to make a telephone call home from the factory. I could see he had cried when he'd told Papa about Mr. Jake.

Raymie said, "Mama's home. Aunt Lucy's gonna be all right."

I was glad to hear such good news, but our bad news was so hurtful I almost forgot to be thankful.

We went through all the matters that needed to be taken care of after a shrimping trip. Mr. Billy Jim came down to oversee his boat being docked.

"Y'all have been through more'n any young folks should," he said, his voice warm with sympathy. He commended us for keeping our heads during such a tragedy. Then he paid us our wages. I was surprised how little the money meant to me now.

Mr. Billy Jim drove us to our homes, even though we lived close by. He said to tell Papa he'd come over to see him later.

"Y'all need a chance to be alone with your folks for a while," he said.

Papa asked a friend to look over things for him at the shop. He came up to the house to be with Mama and us.

Mama and Papa hugged us, and kissed us, and told us they were proud of us. Raymie and I wanted to believe they had reason to be proud, but we couldn't get over the feeling that this had somehow been our fault. Surely we could have gotten to Lissez. Surely we should have insisted we anchor on the bay side.

We told them about Lissez. Papa suggested we all get in the car and go to Dixon's Corner right then. We'd go see Lena and try to find out what she may know about the little boy.

We drove over the dusty lanes to Lena's little house. I always felt sad when we went to Dixon's Corner where the black people lived. The houses were worn and dilapidated. They needed paint. Mama and Lena had talked of ways they might be able to get the county to improve conditions in her community, but they hadn't been able to get much sympathy.

Lena came out to our car.

"Marcie, Raymie, what you all doing home? Oh, my goodness, Miss Helene, did your sister pass on?"

"No, Lena," Mama said. "I came home 'cause she was much better, thank God."

But Lena knew something was wrong. She searched our faces to find the answer.

Papa said, "The kids got caught in a bad squall out in the Gulf, Lena. They think Mr. Jake was drowned."

Her face crumpled in sorrow and disbelief.

"Awww, no, Mr. Isaac, no. I hadn't heard."

"The boat just came in, Lena," Mama explained. "They haven't slept all night. We've come to ask you about a little boy from Dixon's Corner who's missing, too. He'd hidden on the boat—"

"—You gotta mean Ulysses!" Lena exclaimed. "We has reason to believe he was in Bayou La Batre when y'all left. Oh, dear Lawd," Lena said, a prayer in her voice, "he wasn't on the boat, was he? He didn't . . .?"

We all nodded solemnly.

"Y'all come on in. We gotta talk," she said.

I was impressed to see how clean and pretty she kept her house. There were zinnias on the table, and crocheted doilies on the clean but shabby sofa and chairs.

As we talked Lena measured coffee and pumped water. She piled a plate with sliced pound cake, and when the coffee had perked long enough, she poured some for all of us. We showered her with questions about Lissez, and she told us that Ulysses was the son of a cousin who had died when the little boy was born. And she said, yes, it was true, that the boy's daddy hadn't been heard of for a while, but he was a good daddy. No one knew what had happened to him. Many of the neighbors were willing to adopt the boy if anything bad had happened to his daddy.

"Handley and me, we didn't know he was in the truck, for sure. And I can't understand how he got on that boat without all of us seeing him. I feels bad, like it was our fault, Mr. Isaac."

Tears were forming in her large, brown eyes, rolling down her smooth, dark cheeks.

Papa softly said, "Lena, everyone feels guilty, but it ain't anyone's fault. I was down at the shop. I keep wondering why *I* didn't see him. Marcie and Raymie here, they think they could have done something, but it wasn't anyone's fault."

Everyone sat quietly then, thinking and wishing and hoping.

"Lena!" Mama jumped up like a great idea had come to her. "What do you think about having a memorial service together, both our churches, for Mr. Jake and Ulysses?"

Lena shook her head, not sure. She stared out at the woods near her house for a long time. None of us said a word. We were proud of Mama for such a thought, but we weren't as brave about sticking to new ideas as she. I suppose we were afraid of the narrow-minded people who could be unkind.

At last Lena said, "Yes, Ma'am, that would be real nice, but, Miss Helene, they might be trouble with some white folk."

"Maybe. I don't know, Lena, but we can try. Why don't you talk to Brother William over at your church, hmm? And I'll ask Brother Landry. Of all the times we should forget differences, it should be now. Death comes to all of us. The old. The young. The black. The white. The good. The bad."

"Yes, Ma'am, that is sho' true," Lena said.

When we got home Mama said Raymie and I should both take a hot bath, eat a warm breakfast, and get in bed, even though this was the middle of the day.

Once I was snug in the sheets I called, "Good night, Raymie. I love you." I scarcely ever said that to my big brother.

There was no answer. I wanted to hear him say, "I love you, too, Marcie." I couldn't help it; I got up and went to the door separating our rooms and peeked in. His head was back, his eyes closed. He was sound asleep.

I couldn't understand why sleep wouldn't come to me. I was more tired than I ever remembered. I was comfortable. I wasn't hungry.

Mama came to the door. "Why aren't you asleep, Honey?"

"I dunno," I said. "I can't stop thinking."

She came to my bed and sat on the edge, placing her warm hand on my arm.

"I know," she said. Mama could say an "I know" that included and covered everything.

"Mama, do you suppose God was punishing me for being so stubborn about going shrimping?"

"Good, gracious, Marcie. You don't think we have a God who would take the lives of two fine people just to punish you for wanting something so bad, do you?"

"No, Ma'am. But why would he wanna take two nice folks like Mr. Jake and Lissez?"

"Marcie," my wise mama said, "there was a storm. A bad judgment was made that wasn't anyone's fault. How could anyone realize such a bad storm would come up so suddenly? A very little boy, not strong enough to stand the force of such a powerful wind, was washed away. A brave man tried to save him. It's as simple as that. God gave all us humans choices of how to be. But he didn't drown Mr. Jake and your little friend."

"I didn't want them to go," I said, my voice breaking.

When Mama answered, her voice broke, too.

"No, I didn't, either. It's very hard to understand death, but we have to go on, darling."

"I know," I said.

But my "I know" didn't cover or include much of anything.

Mama and Lena

L ife went on in a normal way for the next few
days. On Sunday we went to church, and I
said a special prayer for Mr. Jake and Lissez. On
Monday Raymie and I went back to school. Papa
worked. Mama and Lena kept house. Boats went
out to the Gulf and returned with shrimp and
fish.

There was a difference, though.

When Jeanné and I played, we often stopped
to talk in mournful, whispered tones about Mr.
Jake and the little boy who'd died.

Mama and Lena didn't laugh as they talked.
They spoke only of the memorial service our two
churches were going to have together. They
spoke in soft, murmuring tones, too.

There was talk of some folks disagreeing. A
few people said they "wouldn't be caught dead
going to that funeral." But when our story began

to make the rounds about how Mr. Jake had taken such a "loving" to Lissez, and how that little boy loved Jake and us, too, well, somehow most of the differences seemed to fade away.

Of course, Mama was a big help with that. If anyone so much as mentioned thinking it was "just not right to mix the races that way" she would puff up and tell them what she thought in a language that left no one guessing as to how she felt about God creating us all equal. I guess a person could say my mama was opinionated. I was proud because her opinions had a rightness about them. The interesting thing about it was her way of making other folks think that, "maybe, just maybe, Miss Helene is right."

But the other interesting thing was this. I found that, out in Dixon's Corner where she lived, Lena had the same kind of reputation. Lena and Mama were a good example of people being "soul mates."

Lena didn't deny that a lot of white folks had treated her in a bad way. She didn't go about saying everything was butterflies and roses in her life, but . . .

. . . I heard about something she did say. She told the woman who worked for Dr. Ashland's wife, "You kin say what you wants about all the white folks you wants, but Mr. Jake was a good man, mighty close to an angel. And that precious baby, Ulysses, was an angel. Besides, they both angels now, fo' sure."

People out at the Corner said Lena could get as "riled up" about a matter as Mama when she believed she was right. It looked as if Lena was "opinionated," too.

Mama and Lena figured they'd like to let a few days pass to see if the bodies were found. I suppose they wanted some miracle to happen. But no bodies were found. And no miracles happened.

Mama and Lena said they wanted to be sure every person in Bayou La Batre and Dixon's Corner heard about the memorial service to be held on Wednesday morning at ten o'clock.

The ladies of the two churches had decided to have a lunch after the service so everyone could celebrate the good lives our two friends had lived. I didn't feel like celebrating anything.

Mama knew I was having a hard time. Each night she would talk to me again. I listened, I knew her words were true, but I couldn't understand how she could be planning a celebration at such a time.

"You and Lena act like this is some big party," I told her. "I guess y'all are gonna have ribs and gumbo, tubs of shrimp and lots of cakes. Seems like you wanna make this into some kinda holiday party. Well, it isn't a holiday to me."

Mama said, "Marcie, can't you see? We're celebrating their lives, not their deaths."

I shook my head. It still didn't make sense to me.

Monday afternoon Jeanné and I went to the First Baptist Church in Dixon's Corner while

Mama and Lena talked plans with Brother Williams. We stood around out in the back of the parsonage with Brother Williams's three children.

Melissa, who was my age, said, "You the one knew Lissez?"

"Uh huh," I answered. I felt shy with her. We seldom had the chance to play with the children at Dixon's Corner.

She was as shy as I. She looked down at the ground and drew circles in the dust with her bare toes.

"You like Lissez?" she asked, studying my face with big eyes.

"I only got to know him for a short while," I said, "but I . . . I loved him."

I could see she had to think about this for a long time. She screwed up her face and cocked her head to one side as she asked, "You making a joke?"

I was distressed that she thought I'd joke about such a thing.

"I wanted Mr. Jake to adopt 'im so he could be like my little brother." I was serious; I meant those words with all my heart.

Suddenly she grinned a big, toothy grin. She liked my answer.

"Wanna play hopscotch?" she asked.

"Yeah," I said, grinning back.

Jeanné found a perfect flat piece of green glass. I drew the hopscotch squares with its circle of heaven. For a little while that day I felt a trace of peace.

The next day Jeanné and I went with Mama and Lena while they made plans with Brother Landry and some of the ladies from our church.

While they talked we crossed the road and went across Halbratton's yard to the creek. It was the end of the day, almost dusk. No one was swimming. Jeanné and I sat under the oak tree limb where the boys had hung an inner tube for swinging into the water.

"Would you like to be swimming?" Jeanné asked. "I mean, if we had our bathing suits?"

"Nah," I said. "I don't care if I ever swim again."

I meant it. Nothing seemed the same. I had never seen someone disappear right in front of my eyes, especially someone I had grown to love. I believed I would never get over the horror of that experience.

"But, sometime you'll want to swim again, won't you?" she asked.

"I dunno. I don't think so," I said.

Jeanné felt sorry for me, but she was getting tired of my sadness. She told me so.

"You can't die just 'cause Mr. Jake's gone, you know. I feel bad, too, but aren't you ever gonna laugh and play again? I don't wanna play with you if you're never gonna be happy again."

"Maybe it's 'cause you didn't see it happen, Jeanné," I said. "Maybe it's 'cause Mr. Jake didn't live at your house, but I just can't get over it . . . ever."

I had thought Jeanné would understand. But I suppose she was getting tired of my sadness. She put her hands on her hips in that way she did when she had "had enough."

She said, "Well, other folks feel bad about what happened, too. But everyone's getting sick of the way you never smile anymore. You're not any fun to be with, and I'm going home!"

With that she jumped up and flounced away.

Now I don't even have a friend to play with, I thought. I was miserable with Jeanné, Mama, Lena, everyone. I was especially miserable with myself.

I wandered down to the shop to talk with Papa. I was glad there was no one in the shop with him. I wanted him to comfort me. And I suspect I wanted him to agree with me.

"Papa," I said, "I don't think we should be having a party. I don't wanna go. It's like Mama doesn't even miss Mr. Jake, like she just wants an excuse to have a good time."

"Marcie, did you ever cook for Jake?" Papa asked.

What in the world is he getting at? I wondered.

"No, sir. Well, just on the boat . . ."

"Did you ever wash his clothes for him?"

I was impatient with these silly questions. As far as I was concerned they didn't have anything to do with Mr. Jake dying.

Resentfully, I said, "Well, you know I didn't, Papa."

"How 'bout mending his clothes?"

"Well, no, sir, but I don't think he ever asked me . . ."

Papa looked thoughtful, like he was studying some big question of life.

"Lemme see, now," he said. "When Mr. Jake had the flu last fall, were you the one who took hot soup out to him and went out to read to him while he was getting better?"

"Well, no, but . . ."

". . . Hmmm," Papa said. "I guess Mama knew Mr. Jake about better than all of us, huh? Something else I noticed, too. Last night, when she went to bed, I could hear her crying, sorta soft, like she didn't wanna wake me up."

"She did?" I asked. I hadn't thought of Mama crying, but I wasn't ready to yield to his line of thought. "Well, she doesn't show it. I mean . . ."

Papa put his arm around me. He said, "Y'know, sometimes, it seems to me, that the folks who do all the talking may not feel any worse about things than the ones who put their chins up and do something helpful."

I thought about that for a long time that day. Oh, I knew how much I loved Mr. Jake. I knew I missed him so bad there was an ache in my head, and my stomach, and my heart. But maybe Mama was missing him every bit as much, and she was doing something to show a respect and a caring for him. And for that little boy she'd never even met.

That night, while Mama and Lena were over at the church arranging flowers and vines to make things pretty for the Memorial, I fixed dinner. I cooked all the new things I'd learned to cook on the shrimp trip. I had Raymie run over to Freddie's Fresh Fish House and buy white trout. I used my own money from my piggy bank.

I got to thinking that maybe Papa was right. Mama cared a lot about Jake, but she didn't talk about him every moment. She tried to keep her crying inside while she was *doing* something.

So that's why I fixed dinner on Tuesday night. I learned something else, too. Just like our working on the boat while we were coming home from the shrimp trip had kept us thinking straight, I felt better when I was cooking, setting the table, and washing the dishes.

I felt better, too, when I saw how proud Mama and Papa were at the supper I'd cooked. Even Raymie was proud. He teased me and said the supper was good because *he* had been such a fine teacher.

Surprised, Mama said, "Why, Raymie, you can cook, too?"

That stopped the bragging. He figured working down at the shop for Papa took enough of his time. He didn't want to start cooking, too.

I thought I was learning how to handle my grief, but that night the mournful horn of a shrimp boat heading for the Gulf awakened me. I lay there, remembering our trip, thinking of the things I'd learned, the fun I'd had when all the shrimpers shared their potluck suppers. I remembered Mr. Jolly playing the fiddle and the fellow who almost fell in the hold.

My favorite time had been after we had put Lissez to bed in the pilot house. When Raymie, Hank, Mr. Jake, and I had talked of happy times in our past lives. I thought of how we had made dream plans for the future that included Lissez. Mr. Jake had been happy, thinking about that.

Oh, please, God, I prayed. *Why'd you let this terrible thing happen to us?*

In Memory

Wednesday morning. The cool weather that had come after the squall changed to a pleasant warmness overnight. The April day seemed like the beginning of summer without the southern humidity. I stretched and yawned, feeling well and glad to be alive.

Then I remembered. Mr. Jake. Lissez. This was the day of the Memorial service. In a moment my stomach felt hollow and my heart hurt with sadness again.

I could hear Mama in the kitchen, frying ham and eggs. The mouthwatering smell of ham combined with the appetizing aroma of homemade biscuits drifted into my room.

The day was just beginning. Papa hadn't gone down to the shop yet, and we had the morning off from school to get ready for the service. We ate Mama's tasty breakfast, our usual early morning chatter absent. Each of us was absorbed in his own thoughts.

Mama was rushing about, giving orders.

"Marcie, you wash the dishes and make the beds for me this morning. All right? Isaac, you're closing the shop for two hours, aren't you? Well, you three can come about 9:45. I'm going over about 8:30 with Joanna. Marcie, wear your blue sailor dress, okay?"

Heading for her bedroom, she called back over her shoulder, "Y'all be sure to come sit up front with me, y'hear?"

I tried to keep from thinking while I did the chores Mama had asked me to do. I realized she thought it would be good for me to be busy. She wanted to keep me sane and steady. Yet, somehow, this morning, the lessons I had learned the night before gave me no peace.

I continued to fight the thought of going to a service celebrating Mr. Jake's and Lissez's death. I didn't want to sing hymns of joy and peace when my friends were never going to be with us again. I couldn't see how I would ever be joyful or what good a service would do.

I finished drying the dishes, then put them away on the shelves. I went out to Mr. Jake's shed; I wanted to cry, but the tears wouldn't come. I couldn't understand why the hurt could be so deep in the very heart and soul of me and I couldn't let it out.

I looked at the snapshot of Mr. Jake and his wife in a small frame by his bed. I picked it up and gazed into the smiling face. I looked at the shoes he wore when he gardened. Seeing them made me want to see the garden, so I walked to the rear of our lot. The tomatoes were beginning to ripen. They were large and firm. He would be proud of them.

The tomatoes reminded me of the day I had come to tell him about the possibility of his taking Mr. Billy Jim's boat out. I had stumbled over his tomato strings, and he'd made me feel all right about my clumsiness.

A horrible thought came to me then. I wondered why I hadn't thought of it before.

Why, Mr. Jake would be alive now if I hadn't talked him into going on the trip. Maybe Mr. Tolly would have never thought of asking him after Papa told him about Mr. Jake's bad back. Why, I'd talked him into it! I'd even begged him!

I was certain if I told Mama and Papa about that, they would change their minds about my not being guilty. I went back to his bed and fell across it, my throat aching from unshed tears.

After a while I heard Papa calling me. I realized I had been there for a long time. I hadn't dressed for the service yet.

"I'm coming, Papa. I'll hurry."

When I walked into the kitchen Papa came out, dressed in his blue-and-white striped seersucker suit.

"Aren't you ready, Honey?" he asked.

"I'm sorry," I said. "I'll hurry."

Papa said, "It's all right. We have plenty of time. I came up first while Raymie's minding the store. It's Raymie's turn to dress now. Y'all be ready at 9:45, like your mama said."

As we walked up the path to church, I could see that Raymie was having a hard time, too, but I thought he was lucky. At least he didn't have to blame himself for Mr. Jake's going on the boat.

Under the shade of the huge oak which covered half the lawn of the church were five or six long white tables and a few outdoor cooking stoves. We could hear the strains of Miss Sophia Mae playing "In the Garden."

Inside everyone was wearing his and her best clothes. The women were proper in hats and gloves. Some of the men wore suits but others wore dress shirts and pants with ties and straw hats.

Mama and Lena were ushering the people in, making sure the blacks and whites mingled. The church was quickly filling with men and women, boys and girls of every color. We walked up front to sit at a place Mama had saved for us. Mama and Lena came to join us and Lena's husband, Handley. A handsome young black man sat beside him.

Mama leaned over, and in an urgent whisper she told Papa, "The little boy's father has returned. He'd been in a hospital in St. Louis with pneumonia. Isn't it sad he has to return to this dreadful news?"

Her eyes brimmed with tears.

"It's unfair!" I whispered back.

Mama patted my arm and put her other arm around my shoulder. "I know, honey."

This time I thought, *She can't know*. I didn't believe anyone could know how I felt.

Brother Williams and Brother Landry were seated on the chancel, facing the congregation.

Brother Williams stood and said, "Would you all join me in singing 'A Balm in Gilead'?"

I was sure my heart would break then. Our church had never been this filled. But more important to me, never had these two congregations been joined in this way. And never, never, had the music pealed forth with such power and feeling, the most beautiful music I had ever heard.

I looked about and saw tears rolling down faces of every color, every shade, every tone. There was Lena's handsome face, shining with blackness. Hank sat nearby with his family. After our trip, his face was more freckled than ever. Papa's skin, and Raymie's, too, was tanned but fair. Mama's pale olive skin was almost as dark as Handley's pecan color.

There was something else I noticed. The expressions on the faces of the mourners were peaceful and proud, even as the tears flowed. But Ulysses's daddy broke our hearts. His shoulders shook, trying to control his sobs.

Brother Williams talked of Lissez, how beautiful he was in both appearance and spirit, and he made an attempt to say comforting words to the man who sat beside Handley.

"That little one had a spirit that touched every one of us," he said. He smiled with tenderness at the boy's father. "You can be very proud of him, George Jamison."

I could hear people sobbing. I wanted to sob, too, but I could only feel the solid stone of hurt and anger which had replaced my heart.

Brother Landry talked about Mr. Jake, his forgiving ways, his friendliness, his way of helping everyone.

Father Le Clercq, the priest from St. Bridget's, stood. His church was going to have a special mass for Jake, but he and many of his members were at our memorial service.

Father Le Clercq said, "If Mr. Jake were here he would be proud. This," he said, waving his hand in a gesture to include everyone, "was the way Mr. Jake Brusard felt about the world . . . one world of loving friends."

I knew this fine idea couldn't last. I knew there would be some people who would forget the feeling of being one family of people. But I was proud to know there were people like Mama and Lena who would keep trying.

We had a banquet of singing and praising both God and "the loved ones who have departed from us."

I thought, *Maybe funerals are for people who are left to mourn, not just for the people who died.*

I could see that, as mournful as everyone was, this was a way of saying good-by. Knowing this at the time didn't help, though. I wanted to go home and lie across my bed. I wanted to be alone.

A thought occurred to me. As soon as everyone went to the big luncheon spread out on the tables I would slip away. Maybe no one would miss me in this large crowd.

Brother Landry said, "A wonderful lady is gonna sing for us. When her feast of song is over y'all are invited to join in the feast of lunch the ladies of our two churches have prepared for us."

I was more than surprised when our dear Lena went to the chancel. With great dignity she folded her hands at her waist in a gesture of prayer. In swelling tones she sang "The Lord's Prayer" as Miss Sophia Mae played the piano. I hadn't known Lena could sing like that.

Now everyone was crying. I wanted the tears to come, but I still had a stone where my heart should have been.

Brother Williams stood then and lifted his hands in a gesture of blessing and dismissal.

The service was over. Now would be my chance to leave.

A Miracle?

Figuring out how I could best make my escape, I looked up at the pastors of the two churches. Something was wrong. There were expressions of utter shock on both faces. Brother Williams stood abruptly. He grasped Brother Landry's arm, his mouth open in astonishment.

In the back of the church there was a stirring . . . the sounds of gasps, murmurings of disbelief.

We all turned to see what had happened.

A wonderful sight met our eyes.

Can that possibly be . . . ? Surely I was dreaming. But if this was a dream I never wanted to awaken.

Why, it looks like . . . Mr. Jake. And, yes, Lissez!

And indeed, that's who the bent, exhausted-looking man was. And the boy whose small arms tightly encircled Mr. Jake's neck was Lissez!

The congregation stood in amazement. There was a hubbub of noise and confusion. People began to run to the back of the church. But the strong voice of Brother Landry stopped everyone with a command.

"Brothers and sisters! Please! Give them room!"

Mr. Jake came down the aisle to my mama.

He said, "Miss Helene, we all right. We row home many mile, in fine rowboat Raymie made."

In his eagerness to see his son, George Jamison pushed people aside. He reached out for Lissez as Lissez reached out for him. They hugged one another in a rocking embrace.

I began to sob. At last. That inspiring sight melted the cruel stone. My heart became a heart again.

Papa and Mama hugged me, and Raymie joined in. Papa pulled Mr. Jake into our hug.

Mama pulled away first. She took Mr. Jake's arms and insisted he sit down. It was obvious to everyone the man was ill with exhaustion.

"Oh, you poor dears," Mama said. "We have to take care of you right now."

Well, there's a lot to tell about that reunion. Of course, everyone was excited and thrilled. We huddled around the two survivors, astounded, dumbfounded, but thankful. We were almost hysterical with relief.

The ladies saw to it that Mr. Jake and Lissez were welcomed like the heroes they were. Blankets were brought forth from somewhere, and makeshift beds were soon made under the oak. Food and drink were brought to them. Mr. Jamison sat on the blanket with Lissez lying across his lap. I have never seen anyone as happy as Lissez, unless it was his daddy.

On all sides the questions flew, like a mad assortment of birds darting this way and that. Mr. Jake and Lissez were confused by the commotion. Eventually, Mr. Jake, through weak laughter, said, "If you happy for us, you must eat, too. Then I answer questions plenty."

He waved a feeble hand toward the tables. We realized, then, that we weren't allowing them to eat.

Embarrassed, he shook his head unbelievingly. "Much, much food. I never think I see again. *Merci beaucoup a le bon Dieu* (Many thanks to the good God)," he said.

He explained everything to his astonished audience. He and Lissez had fallen near the skiff, and when Hank had beamed the light on them, they were under the skiff. Jake had been certain they would both drown. When he'd come up, choking, he tried to call but the force of the waves and Lissez's arms tightly clutching his throat in terror made calling impossible.

He told how he had, against all odds, righted the boat and pulled the almost drowned little boy into it.

Shaking his head, he said, "We row to island, but we must be on other end. We not see you."

116

"Only God give de strength. Back strong. Thinking strong."

They had stayed on the island a few days to gain strength for the row back. He had found oysters near the marsh, and they had eaten them . . . the only food they'd had.

Finally he decided to start home in the skiff. Fortunately the two oars were still attached to their hooks, something difficult to believe when he first discovered it. Also, he couldn't understand why he hadn't seen other shrimp boats. Eventually, as they entered the mouth of the bayou, his friend, Luis Delacruz, with Pierre and his brother, had found them.

"He want take us to house—or de city, Mobile to hospital, but we hear from other shrimper about memory service for dead *M'sieu* Jake and Lissez. We not want a service for dead peoples who much, much alive."

Lissez reached over and patted Mr. Jake's back, and I had to swallow hard to keep from sobbing in joy when Lissez's daddy reached over and patted Mr. Jake's tired, bent back, too.

Mr. Jake was as interested as we to hear why Lissez's father, George Jamison, had been missing, so he asked Mr. Jamison to tell his story.

Mr. George had been in St. Louis for many days. In the past he had worked as a carpenter, so he tried to get work with construction companies, but there was nothing to be found. The weather was cold, and he had to sleep on the

117

streets. He caught pneumonia and awakened in a hospital.

We wondered how he had gotten out, and especially, how he had gotten home.

"My mama, she have a third cousin in Alton, Illinois. She come to the hospital and bought me a ticket home. I's mighty thankful to the good Lawd I's home again with my boy. And I will never forget to lift my voice in praise that my baby boy is alive."

Amazing wonders continued. Mr. Ham Snivelly asked George to come work for him at his shipyard. He said he'd help him to learn how to make boats.

"It ain't much different from building houses," he said.

Lissez said, "If we ain't gonna move to St. Louis I kin get t'see Mr. Jake and play with Marcie."

I beamed all over.

Mr. Jake was as pleased as I, but Lissez's daddy hesitated. I suspected he knew there were a lot of white folks who hated black folks, and maybe he was thinking of the black people who hated white people, too.

I looked down at my lap, my now softened heart hurting. I felt bad for everyone, and I was embarrassed and angry for the narrow people who hurt other folks like that.

My mama kneeled on the blanket by George Jamison. She placed her gentle hands on Lissez's shoulders.

"You mighty right, Lissez," she softly murmured. "You can come to see us anytime you want, darling."

Then she looked at George Jamison and smiled. "And you're just as welcome as he is."

Well, I'd like to think everything changed in our town after that. There were still people who thought mama was some kind of "freak" for being friends with black folks. Some of them were even mean to her.

But luckily, there weren't that many snobbish people in our town. Mama said that was because most of us were kind of poor, not much better off than the blacks. There weren't any plantations. Many people of both races worked together in the shrimp factories and canneries. And although there weren't a lot of Cajuns in our town, something of the Cajun acceptance of all peoples had probably rubbed off on the people of Bayou La Batre. That may have been partly why Mama felt that way. She'd grown up among Cajuns in Louisiana.

After that, ever so often, on a Sunday afternoon, George Jamison brought Lissez to see Mr. Jake and me. I think Mr. Jake was a little disappointed he wouldn't be able to adopt Lissez the way he'd hoped, but of course he knew this was best, and I'm sure he was happy Lissez had his own papa.

There were a million, jillion things to think about after that shrimping trip. I learned to have a new respect for my big brother, I learned to do some practical things I'd never have learned at home, and I made a new little friend.

I learned about death and how it brought people together in a sweet and wonderful way, even though we were "mightily blessed," as Lena said, that our terrible tragedy turned out so well. I learned that funerals and memorials are for the living, loving folks who are left behind to have a chance to say good-bye.

I learned about miracles.

I had a long talk with Mama and Papa about miracles. One night at supper I told them, and Raymie, that I didn't understand why we didn't have miracles "in modern times."

"I don't even think I believe in miracles," I said. I thrust out my lip.

I'd been thinking about the story in the Bible about the loaves and fishes, and I was having a hard time believing "that stuff," as I called it.

Mama said, "Oh, is that right? Well, what about the miracles that happened to me? Twice. Do you know about that?"

"No, Ma'am," I said, wondering what she was trying to prove.

"First, the day a fine baby boy was born to your father and me. Then, four years later, how 'bout the precious baby girl who came to us? Two miracles."

"Oh, Mama!" I said, liking what she was saying but feeling unsure about birth being a miracle.

Papa's eyes twinkled when he said, "I think it was a miracle the day Miss Meticulous Marcie gutted a fish."

They all laughed.

I gave his hand a playful slap and giggled. "Papa!"

But he was serious when he said, "And how about George Jamison, almost dying in a hospital and finding a cousin who could help him out?"

"That wasn't a *miracle*," I said. "That was luck."

Mama put a hand on my arm. She smiled at me, but I could see she was dead serious as she said, "Luck, hmm? Well, it isn't easy to apply a miracle to oneself, but I have never seen such a wonderful miracle as the one you were given."

"What miracle?" I asked, "No miracle has ever happened to me, that's for sure."

"Why, Marcie Delchamps!" she scolded. "You and Raymie and Hank were all part of a miracle. You were able to brave that storm and get to the other side of Bird Island."

"That's a miracle?"

Raymie surprised me by speaking out, "Yeah, 'cause I don't know how we did it. And how about Mr. Jake and Lissez, coming through that storm and having the strength to row that little skiff home? That was really something! That musta been a miracle."

Mama gave a happy little laugh as she said, "Yes! And have you ever seen a more beautiful miracle of creation than that little 'ghost,' Ulysses S. Jamison?"

I thought about this for a long time before I answered, "Maybe I do believe in miracles."

A tiny imp of mischievousness prompted me to add, "And you know something? I think it was a stupendous, amazing, incredible miracle that convinced Mama, and Papa, and Raymie, and Mr. Jake, and that silly teaser, Mr. Billy Jim Boisonot, to let a little piker shrimp of a girl like me be part of a shrimping crew."

Everybody laughed.

About the Author

Betty Hager tells us that she never got to take a trip on a shrimp boat, but as a child she did swim and crab in the bay near her hometown in Alabama. She did row a skiff on the bayou. And she did take boat rides on the Gulf of Mexico. In addition, Betty's mother, like Marcie's, believed in the dignity of all people and taught Betty to treat everyone with love and respect.

Betty was eight years old when she became hooked on writing. Although she majored in writing at the University of Alabama, she didn't pursue her writing in earnest until years later. When the youngest of her three sons graduated from high school, she wrote *Old Jake and the Pirate's Treasure* and also began to write children's musicals.

Marcie and the Shrimp Boat Adventure is the third book in the Tales from the Bayou series. Betty hopes you will read all four books about Marcie and her older brother, Raymie.

Betty loves to hear from her readers. You may write her at this address:

Betty Hager
Author Relations
Zondervan Publishing House
Grand Rapids, MI 49530

Look for more of Marcie's adventures!

Old Jake and the Pirate's Treasure
Book 1 $4.99 0-310-38401-X

Is Old Jake really hiding a pirate's treasure map?
Marcie, Raymie, and Hank decide to find out —
by sneaking inside Old Jake's house! They're on
to a mystery and more ...

Miss Tilly and the Haunted Mansion
Book 2 $4.99 0-310-38411-7

Marcie imagines all sorts of things, like maybe
Miss Tilly really is a witch. When her mother
makes her visit Miss Tilly, some terrifying
adventures and a new friend await her ...

Marcie and the Shrimp Boat Adventure
Book 3 $4.99 0-310-38421-4

Marcie's brother gets to do so much — like go
sailing on the shrimp boat. So when Marcie finally
gets on board, she's overjoyed. But soon she finds
she needs a miracle to get out alive ...

Marcie and the Monster of the Bayou
Book 4 $4.99 0-310-38431-1

Marcie is sure she saw a monster, but the only
person who doesn't laugh is also telling awful
stories about Marcie's new friend. Soon Marcie
must face a bigger enemy — a hurricane.